CINNAMON

OTHER BOOKS BY JANET MASON

THEY: A Biblical Tale of Secret Genders (2018)
The Unicorn: The Mystery (2020)
Available at Adelaide Books, amazon.com, barnesandnoble.com and other

online and some local retailers

Cinnamon
a dairy cow's (and her farmer's) path to freedom

by award-winning author
JANET MASON

ADELAIDE BOOKS
New York / Lisbon
2024

CINNAMON: A dairy cow's (and her farmer's) path to freedom
a novel by
Janet Mason

Copyright © 2024 by Janet Mason

Published by Adelaide Books, New York / Lisbon
adelaidebooks.org

Editor-in-Chief
Stevan V. Nikolic

All rights reserved. No part of this book may be reproduced in any manner whatsoever without written permission from the author except in the case of brief quotations embodied in critical articles and reviews.

For any information, please address Adelaide Books
at info@adelaidebooks.org

ISBN 13: 978-1-958419-78-6

Printed in the United States of America

*To Barbara, who introduced me to Sacred (the cow),
who changed our lives.*

To Leona —

Enjoy!

Janet
2025

Contents

Chapter One *9*

Chapter Two *11*

Chapter Three *20*

Chapter Four *27*

Chapter Five *38*

Chapter Six *47*

Chapter Seven *57*

Chapter Eight *67*

Chapter Nine *77*

Chapter Ten *89*

Chapter Eleven *99*

Chapter Twelve *104*

Chapter Thirteen *113*

Chapter Fourteen *116*

Chapter Fifteen *125*

Chapter Sixteen *127*

Chapter Seventeen *139*

Chapter Eighteen *151*

Chapter Nineteen *162*

Chapter Twenty *173*

Chapter Twenty-One *178*
Chapter Twenty-Two *189*
Chapter Twenty-Three *196*
Chapter Twenty-Four *205*
Chapter Twenty-Five *218*
Chapter Twenty-Six *233*
Chapter Twenty-Seven *242*
Chapter Twenty-Eight *252*
Chapter Twenty-Nine *261*
Chapter Thirty *268*
About the Author *279*

Chapter One

Wow! Look at her go! She should have a racing stripe down that fork. Not to mention how she shovels it in. I've seen farmers bale less hay before it was done by machines. I could stand here until the chair under her collapsed if I had the time. And they call cows fat!

I swatted a fly with my tail nonchalantly as I looked through the window at the farmer. I had snuck out of the pasture and was spying on our captor. I kept peering into the window until I saw another person standing in front of the stove. The back of the shirt was a mixture of sky blue and deep violet. It was the color of a periwinkle flower I had eaten.

Still sitting at the table, the farmer turned toward me. I ducked my head and followed the light fragrant scent of a white daisy.

Chomp. Chomp. Chomp.

Without thinking about it, I went from smelling the daisy to eating it. The bristly yellow center tasted slightly bitter. The pure white petals tasted so sweet it was like eating goodness.

Mmmm.

I was so hungry even the center tasted good as I finished it off.

It didn't look like there were any other flowers left to eat. There had been a few others, but I ate them earlier. I got bored waiting with my head down, so I nosed around and found three more daisies I hadn't seen before! I ate them immediately. People think that we're chewing our cuds. But maybe we're munching on secret things the humans don't know we're eating, like carefully tended flowers.

I probably ate too much in those days. I'd been trying to cut back and eat less of the feed they gave us in the barn and eat less grass. But I always eat more when I let myself become ravenous. This time, I joked to myself that I was so hungry that I could eat a human. Then I felt nauseous. I don't know if it was hunger or the thought of eating a human that made me feel queasy. The feeling passed, and I ate the flowers.

I figured if I slimmed down, I wouldn't have to be milked so often. Maybe the farm hands would overlook me when it came time for inseminating us so that we could give them more calves to make milk. I'm sick of the farmhand's entire arm going up my you know what. That's only a little better than when they used to bring the male cows in to hump us. Apparently, that didn't work, so the farmhands got involved.

Chapter Two

The next day, I heard a young cow emit a long whimper.

She had given birth just the other day – and had been sighing ever since.

I was facing the opposite direction in my slot in the barn, but had my ears turned back so that I could hear everything.

The cow in the last place next to her stall told the new mother that if she didn't get up, the farmhands would assume she was sick and send her away.

"And then what?" asked the young mother.

Her voice was distant. It sounded as though she was still lying in the stall that was at the end of the long area where we stood side by side in a line when we were hooked up to the milking machines.

I had seen her just minutes before, when I had been herded to my milking space, which was much narrower than the birthing stall. I imagined her big brown eyes looking up inquisitively as she spoke.

"Will they send me somewhere special and help me get better?" she asked plaintively.

"They'll send you someplace special for sure – the slaughterhouse," the standing cow replied, with the deeper voice of the two.

I remembered her as black and white but mostly black around the shoulders and face. with black spots dotting her white mid-section.

"My advice is to toughen up. They're going to keep you pregnant for as long as they can so that you provide them with milk."

"How long will that last?"

The new mother with the higher voice sounded young. This must be her first time giving birth. I felt sorry for the poor thing. I was still standing in my slot on the other side of the aisle and had already been hooked up to the machine to be milked, so I couldn't turn around.

The standing cow with the deeper voice sounded like she had been around for a while. I strained to hear what she had to say.

"After we give birth, we can produce milk for close to a year. So, it's a long time," said the standing cow.

"I guess that's the amount of time I should have been with my baby," sniffed the younger cow. "I was barely able to lick off the placenta before they whisked him or her away."

"Oh. It must have been a boy," said the cow with the deeper voice.

"Whatever do you mean?" The younger cow's voice was suddenly higher.

"I didn't mean anything," said the cow with the deeper voice. "I was just speculating."

I surmised that the older more experienced cow, as jaded as she seemed, didn't want to tell the young cow that if her calf was male, he would be sent away immediately.

"We're pregnant for nine months," said the cow with the deeper voice. "That's almost a year and it's a long time to be carrying our young. Of course, we develop feelings for our calves when they're still inside of us."

The other cow whimpered.

"That's why I feel so badly," she said sadly.

"Of course, you feel bad," replied the older cow. "We all feel bad. It doesn't help to wallow in your pity. Stand up and be counted. Instead of feeling sorry for yourself, do something to change your circumstances," said the older cow with an edge of irritation.

Her tone wasn't lost on me. It seemed like the young cow heard it too.

"But what should I do?" The young cow's higher voice trembled.

"If I knew the answer, would I be standing here?" The older cow with the deeper voice snorted and then said, "You have to figure it out for yourself. I can't do it for you."

"It might help if I knew what was going to happen to me next," said the younger cow.

"*If* you stand up, the farmhands will assume you're healthy. Then they try to make sure you get pregnant again – and you hope you do …"

"Why would I do that?"

Youngsters are apt to be impertinent, and this one was turning out to be no different.

"So, you can give them what they want – more milk. This will buy you more time to figure out what to do before it's too late." I heard the dullish stamping of hooves against dirty straw and cement. The cow who was talking must be stamping her feet in frustration.

"Do I have to tell you everything?" the standing cow asked with an edge in her voice.

"I'm afraid you do," answered the new mother. "There was an older cow whom I used to stand next to when I grew big enough to go to the pasture. She was like a mother to me. I was taken from my own mother. I assumed something happened to her."

"All of us have been taken from our mothers. Hopefully, your mother was able to get pregnant at least two more times and give milk for almost a year between each pregnancy. Then she would've gotten sent away."

The sound of the standing cow's voice was kinder.

"Sent away? – That doesn't sound so bad. Where did they send her?" asked the young cow with the higher voice. I heard hope in her voice.

The older cow sighed. It didn't sound like she was going to try to sugarcoat her answer.

"Whenever you hear the term 'sent away,' it's never good. It almost always means that someone is going to the slaughterhouse. We all get sent away eventually. Most of us get eaten by the humans."

"Ohhh," whimpered the young cow. "How terrible."

Even standing behind them, I felt the sadness in the young mother's whimper.

"But you're still young," said the standing cow. Her deeper voice softened with compassion.

"Maybe your mother's still here…"

The older one was silent for a moment as if considering not saying what followed.

"There's even a chance that I'm your mother."

"Oh?" said the younger one.

"Don't get your hopes up," said the standing one rather crossly. "I can't make everything better. And it's too late for me to nurture you. All I can tell you is to stand up before one of the farmhands reports that you're sick – and you get sent away."

"I *am* young. I bet I'm the youngest one in this section of the barn. My play mother/friend in the pasture was very sweet. She never would have told me such horrible things."

The milking machine chugged away. It was the only sound in the air. I could feel the tension under the mechanical sound. The older, more experienced cow probably felt insulted. I imagined that she was thinking the horrible things she told the younger one were true. Her only crime was telling the truth.

What she had said sounded right to me. I had given birth twice and was used to the milking machine. I was horrified at the thought that I only had a few years left – *if* I could get pregnant again. But a year was a long time and two years – well, I knew enough math to know that two years was twice as long.

I still felt bad for the young mother. I didn't feel any less bad for her because she had insulted her elder. She was too young to know that insulting someone wasn't going to change her reality. I knew that even if the young cow was too inexperienced to know much.

There were some interesting-looking yellow grains on the concrete floor outside of my area. It looked like some feed had spilled on the floor. I could hear the sighs of relief as the others down the line were unhooked from the milking machine. I would be unhooked from the milking machine soon. I thought about kneeling after I was unhooked from the milking machine so I could reach it with my long tongue but sighed. Even if the grain was good, what was the point?

Eating the yummy-looking grain wouldn't change anything.

Despite my lethargy, I began to think of what I could say, when I walked by after I was unhooked from the milking machine on my way out of the barn, to make the young mother feel better. Finally, the farmhand took the clamps off me. Relief. I backed up and walked by the stall with the young cow in it. I noticed that she had taken the older cow's advice and was standing.

"Don't worry," I murmured when I walked by.

There was much to worry about. I felt ashamed that I hadn't been honest with the young mother.

I stopped and looked down.

The straw under my feet was filled with dung. This wasn't unusual.

Lately, there was more dung than hay. I had heard one of the farmhands – the one who traveled with a ham sandwich in the front of his overalls – claim that he had cleaned out our barn when he had done no such thing. I assumed he hadn't felt like it the first time. Then when he found he could get away with it, not cleaning out the barn became a habit.

Even though it stank to the high heavens, I lowered my head to my front leg as if I were scratching my leg with my nose so I could speak to the young mother.

"It will be okay. When you leave the barn – in a week or so after you're done milking – you will pass by the calves' stall at the other end of the barn. It's always good to see them even if your little one was already sent away. Don't worry, you will have another one."

I stood up and looked over quickly as I stood waiting in line to get out of the barn and be herded into the pasture. The young cow looked determined – suddenly strong like young mothers often look. I noticed that her legs were still spindly. She almost looked like a calf herself.

As the line started to move, I still felt a little guilty. I hadn't been able to tell the young cow the truth. I just told her what she needed to hear to go on with her life. But it wasn't the entire story. Hamburger. Steaks. It's all the same thing to me. I've heard the term "beef cattle" used but I call it what it is: murder.

That's how we lived our lives then. But at the same time, there was our daily reality of breathing in and breathing out while we stood in a rolling green pasture. Sometimes we were doing other things too.

Chapter Three

I got bored and snuck out of the pasture again.

Since I had almost gotten caught last time, I was extra careful when I spied on our captor in the farmhouse.

I had reasons for my spying – other than boredom.

I figured I might learn a thing or two from our captor. Maybe I would learn the answer to how we could get free. But to tell you the truth, I spied on the farmer because I was intrigued by her.

I knew she had her limitations – she was human after all – but I wanted to find everything out about her that I could.

I took care because I didn't want her to catch me watching and send me back to the pasture – or worse yet, back to the crowded and smelly barn. It was still morning. A certain silence hung in the air under the hum of cicadas. The plants were still dewy with possibility (even if it was just going turn into another day or worse) – and it was drawing close to the first milking time of the day. Those mechanical milking machines that they hooked us up to in those days were painful, not to mention cold!

They say cows are dumb animals. It's true we're animals. Aren't we all? But we're not dumb in the sense of being stupid like human animals. We might be dumb in the sense that we are unwilling to talk – most of us are too angry to speak, especially to humans. But we grumble among ourselves, and we warn other animals – including birds – when they need to be warned.

I was still bored. Even though I had escaped from the pasture and was outside of the farmhouse where I could spy on the farmer, it felt like I had been standing out in nature for an eternity and nothing had changed. But the fact is that a lot had changed. For one thing, I was suddenly surrounded by machines that creaked and wheezed. The humans used to wheeze too. But at least it was an animal sound. That meant there was always the chance they would recognize they weren't that different than us. However, the machines didn't know a thing!

I sniffed the air and swatted a fly with my tail. I'm a Jersey cow – so I've heard -- which is why I'm a copper color instead of being black and white like most of the cows who were in the pasture and the barn. I noticed over the last six months or so that there seemed to be a shift in consciousness. The grumbling of the cows was, at times, deafening. The birds that sat above on the wire – like clothespins on a line – told me that all the humans hear is loud mooing. But there was rebellion in the air. Just last week, several of the younger cows escaped and ran out onto the road. I overheard the farmhands laughing and talking when they brought the cows back. One farmhand said to the other that the cows must have hidden behind a truck or a tractor and then escaped when the gate was raised.

The other farmhand said that the cows were lucky they weren't hit by one of the vehicles zooming by on the road. What a mess that would've been! Metal and flesh everywhere! It wouldn't have mattered who the flesh belonged to. Flesh is flesh, right? But the rebellion wasn't going to work that way. I knew it even then. I could feel it in my bones as I observed and strategized, thinking *there has to be a way to get out of here. There must be a place to go.*

But I had to admit I liked it here. The rolling green pasture was home to me. I knew its nooks and crannies – where the cleanest spurts of water came from, where the tastiest grasses grew, and the best places to prance with my friends. And my friends were there!

I even liked it when the farmer came to visit, when I poked my head under the top rail of the wooden fence, and she petted my long nose from behind my big nostrils to the soft place between my eyes just the way I liked it. I liked the barn – even though I complained about it being cramped and smelly. It had the potential to be a decent place. There were hoot owls who lived in a nearby tree. Their reassuring calls lulled us to sleep. We could even see when the moon was full because its splash of white light came through the opening high at the end of the barn. If it had been cleaned regularly so that it had more straw than dung in it, the barn would have been pleasant. But it wasn't. Plus, there were too many of us cows in too small of a place. There was no room to spread out and dream.

I didn't hold it against the farmer, though. I liked her. She was bright and sunny. She always had a good word. But as I learned more about what happened to us, I began to think of her as our captor. Still, I thought if I learned more about her it might help.

That's why I was standing there – an escapee from the pasture – spying on my captor. The coast was clear. I moved over a few steps to the right so I could look back into the window of the farmhouse. The farmer was sitting at the table with her eyes closed. She seemed to be inhaling the aroma from several red and white strips on her plate. The person standing behind her at the stove had turned around again and faced away from me to the stove. With a swat of my tail on my other side (it felt like another fly), I wondered briefly if the person at the stove was male or female. Was the person a husband, a partner, or both? He or she appeared to be some sort of companion who liked to feed the farmer.

I realized that it didn't matter. My world of us and them has always been almost genderless (except for the poor male calves). There are basically only humans and bovines – that is human animals and bovine animals. Even if we are, in many ways, the same – we are still very different. For one thing, bovines don't eat humans. And we don't lock them in the pasture or the smelly barn.

I assumed because the woman at the table lived in the farmhouse that she must own the farm. But did she own me? Maybe she just thought that she owned me. Perhaps she'll come to realize that she was mistaken. After all, can one animal really own another one?

I think not.

The house cat found the red-and-white strip of flesh on the farmer's plate to be very interesting. The orange fluff ball bounded up from the floor onto the table beside the captor's plate and sniffed. I saw the cat part his or her lips and stick out a pink tongue. That fast, the captor shoved the cat off the table.

Through the closed window, I heard the captor exclaim: "Bad kitty. I told you, Tangerine, no jumping on the table!"

Then the cat jumped from the floor to the table again and my captor said, "Good jumper, Tangerine! Well, I guess you deserve a treat for that."

Then my captor held out the strip of flesh to the cat who eagerly nibbled on it.

I found the scene confusing, even if it was the cat who was getting mixed messages. My captor couldn't even stand up to a cat!

I widened my nostrils and took a deep inhale of the sweet and tangy scented air. Bacon! The dead-flesh scent had drifted out of the house making me forget why I had taken my deep breath. I was going to wish my fellow creatures well – as I exhaled. But when I discovered what she was eating I decided to forget about wishing her well. BACON!!

I've heard that humans like to eat pigs and call the strips of flesh bacon but have never seen it before. I had just smelled it one morning in the pasture when my cow friend from childhood remarked, "Oh, the smell of bacon is particularly strong today." Then she proceeded to tell me what bacon was. When I looked horrified, she said simply, "Don't worry, I never heard of cows being turned into bacon."

"As if that solves the problem," I had retorted.

But my friend had already turned away and was headed to the bales of hay. It did look sweet that day – all light and clean as if the baler had picked it especially for us. But I didn't join my friend. How could she eat after what she just told me?

Don't get me wrong. I was relieved that the human on the other side of the window wasn't eating a cow. After all, the strips of flesh could come from us. I hadn't heard of cow bacon, but that didn't mean that it didn't exist. If people eat us in other ways – I'm sure it wouldn't be that hard to make bacon from us too. We're not that different from pigs, after all.

I've always been as self-absorbed as the next creature. It's a cow-eat-cow world. But how would the human like it, if I were to eat one of her friends?!

"Well, there goes Martha," she would say, maybe adding, "I never liked her anyway." Or perhaps she would say, "It's a shame, but I bet she tastes too good not to be eaten."

Or maybe she would be outraged like me.

Chapter Four

It was Sunday morning – the next day. After Ainsley made me a big breakfast, I did what I always do on Sunday mornings. I got dressed for church. I thought about asking Ainsley to go with me, but knew the habitual response would be a cheerful, "No thanks hon, but thanks for asking."

I dressed extra carefully that morning and took my new to me pecan brown leather handbag. When I left the house, I noticed one of the brown cows was outside of the pasture. She looked familiar. I assumed she was the cow I petted and talked to frequently. I walked over to her and petted her large wet nose and rubbed her soft fur the way I knew she liked it – to the spot that felt like velvet just between her big brown eyes.

She nuzzled me, just the way I had taught her. Then she sniffed my leather bag.

"So, you like my new purse?" I asked.

I knew she couldn't understand me, but it was nice to have *some* validation. Ainsley hadn't said a word about my purse and acted as if I should be happy just having someone to cook me pancakes and bacon in the morning. To tell you the truth, I was happy. I knew I was lucky. And I was grateful. I hummed a little as the cow sniffed my purse. Then I looked back into the cow's eyes and saw the look. I stopped humming.

The look the cow gave me was cold and hard. Her eyes narrowed and became glassy. The air between us seemed to crackle. She didn't need to speak to tell me she felt betrayed. She had made her feelings known. At first, I thought I was imaging things. I immediately felt guilty. I thought about the fact that she was brown, and my purse was brown. But her fur was brown, and my purse was leather. Leather! What was I thinking? I could be wearing the hide of her cousin!

I felt a little crazy thinking I could interpret the feelings of one of my cows. I did feel close to her. I figured it was okay since she was a dairy cow. It wasn't as though we were going to sell her for slaughter like one of the pigs! At least this was the argument that I gave Ainsley who often suggested that I not get too close to the farm animals. "But," Ainsley had said and then hesitated and said nothing. I said nothing in return. We both knew what happened to the dairy cows when they were "sent away" but we didn't talk about it. I got to thinking that maybe Ainsley was right. Perhaps I did need to get out more.

That's why I decided to start going to a nearby church on Sunday mornings. I had just started going to church last year, but already it felt like a second home to me – somewhere I was meant to be. I was headed there now, but first I had to lead the cow back to the pasture. I steered clear of the electric wire guard that ran from the fence on the top to the latched gate. Then I unlatched the wooden gate. A younger cow who I had named Star – because she had a white star shape in the short black fur of her forehead – was grazing nearby the rusted jug handle where fresh water came out of the ground like a fount. Since it was Sunday, I had only had one farm hand come in and only for a few hours around the milking times. It was quiet without the clacking of the machines.

I still felt silly about thinking I could tell what the cow was feeling. I also felt guilty for feeling guilty. As I stood on the other side of the open gate and coaxed the cow back into the pasture, it came to me that I might have imagined the look because I felt guilty that I hadn't even named this cow I was fond of.

"Come on, Elsie," I said sweetly.

The cow glowered at me and stubbornly stood still. I suddenly understood the phrase, "digging in your heels."

I decided I was going to have to do better. Maybe Elsie was too common of a name – maybe this cow knew that the name was already taken and was in its own way a second-hand name even if the Elsie of Borden-fame was a cartoon.

"How now brown cow," I said, elongating the vowels.

The cow still didn't budge. Instead, she gave me what I thought was an unusually aggressive stare – for a cow. She pawed the ground and snorted like a bull.

This cow, apparently, was not interested in elocution lessons.

My adrenaline was flowing. I thought fast. She was a beautiful color – like fresh cinnamon grated into a latte. Not that I did any grating, of course, since that was Ainsley's department.

Maybe the cow wanted a name about something that was distinctive about her – like her color. I had thought that she looked a little put out when she heard me address Star by her name. But, again, I thought I had imagined that.

I looked deep into her large brown eyes.

"I'm sorry about the leather purse," I said.

I still felt silly thinking that I could understand what the cow felt, or that she could understand me. But since there was no one else around, I decided to honor my own emotions – even if I believed them foolish.

I was still standing in the pasture but on the other side of the wooden gate.

"Come on Cinnamon," I coaxed.

It felt funny calling a cow Cinnamon. I could just hear Ainsley saying that "Cinnamon" was a name you would call a stripper, not a dairy cow. But a little voice inside me told me that "Cinnamon" was her name, so I stuck with it.

"I named you 'Cinnamon' because you're a beautiful shade of light brown that could only be described as an exotic spice that people commonly use but rarely think about."

I pursed my lips and made the cow-coaxing sounds with my tongue (cluck, cluck, cluck) that I know they like.

"Come on Cinnamon," I said softly, lovingly. "There's fresh water and bales of hay in here especially for you."

She dropped her aggressive look but, staying planted where she was, looked doubtful. I owned a whole barnful of cattle that came out here to graze at different times. Truth be told, I didn't think only of Cinnamon when I brought the feed. I thought of all my cows. I thought about how much grass and feed they had to consume to produce milk. I thought about how my investment in the higher protein grains – such as the alfalfa and soy grasses – were worth it. I did not think only about the cow who I had just named.

Apparently, Cinnamon came with a built-in bull-shit detector.

"There's plenty of tasty grass to snack on and" – I motioned to the long green rolling hill behind me that dipped into the fenced-in line of green deciduous trees behind it. It looked so bucolic, especially since it was quiet on Sunday when there were fewer machines making their clacking noises. At present, there were no machines operating. A few unseen birds chirped from the branches of leafy trees. The wire the birds usually sat on was empty (something must have scared them into the trees) and their casual chirping was the extent of the sound out here. It made me understand the saying, "Silence is golden." I remembered to finish my thought, "Plus there's a patch of clover – and other white flowers, maybe they are daisies – near the forest."

At that, Cinnamon bounded through the wooden gate into the pasture.

That's the story of how Cinnamon got her name and how we started our friendship.

As I walked out of the pasture and secured the wooden gate behind me, I looked at the sloping pasture and listened to the deep-throated chirps of the birds. I looked up at the cyan sky dotted with a few white, cirrus clouds the wind had elongated like vanilla taffy on a stick.

I remembered the day in high school when I learned from the wizened English teacher – Miss Turpin – that the word bucolic came from the Latin word *bucolicus* which means "cowherder."

Miss Turpin, who at the time was older than God (that's the way she described herself – without so much as a chuckle), rested her dark beady eyes on me and bestowed me with one of her smiles – rare coming from her shoe-leather face.

She was so short that she was my height when I was sitting down, so when I smiled back at her we were both at the same level. She may have sensed something about me – in bestowing a future on me where I would have what I wanted. For as long as I remember, I have loved cows.

I was one of the lucky ones in that my parents gave me their farm. I'm an only child so there wasn't anyone else to take over the farm or to divide up the parcel of land and to sell off their part. My parents did this a few years ago when they had enough of farming and moved to a retirement home. Papa has since passed. He died, like he had lived, with a cigarette in his hand. He had emphysema.

Lots of people think that smoking is a disgusting habit. There's no doubt that it is addictive. Papa told me many times that he wished he never started because he couldn't quit. He started smoking when he was in college and then kept it up for the fifty years when he was an accountant for a large grain company – almost the same amount of time that he ran the farm. Like many farmers, he had several occupations.

Maybe smoking is also disgusting – besides being the thing that kept him going. But there was something comforting, too, about my Papa's cigarette smoke – especially when I woke up early and smelled it. I knew the smoke from Papa's cigarette was trailing into the sunrise. The smell of smoke let me know Papa was there.

Mama was still living then. I was worried about her at first – especially after Papa died. How was she going to go on without him? But she was extremely faithful to her canasta card group she met with each week at the home. She also took the senior bus on day trips – like visits to the shopping mall and to the caverns. The caverns cater to the tourists and are about twenty-minutes outside of town. Mama told me that the caverns have an even walkway and good handrails for the seniors. At the home, Mama ate dinner with the other older women who had lost their spouses. All that socializing seemed to keep her going.

Before Papa died, my parents told me that a farmer's life was hard and getting harder. They suggested that I sell the land and set myself up in business. I protested. Where would I go? Everything was so expensive. I couldn't imagine selling the land to a developer or to someone planning to frack the land for oil and gas. I had heard there were so many bad side effects from fracking it could not only hurt this land but the land around it. I couldn't live with that. I also couldn't live with the thought of another strip mall. But they were the only ones offering good prices for land. Other farmers were mostly struggling too much to be able to afford more land. Besides, I didn't want to sell the land. The farm was my heritage. I had sprung from the same land that the cows grazed on. I knew someday, the land would be part of my memory of Mama and Papa.

My parents saw my point. I think now they were touched. They suggested I turn the old farmhouse into a bed and breakfast and maybe rent out the land to another farmer. They told me it was hard to run a bed and breakfast, that it is a twenty-four hour a day job. But they also told me that running a farm would be harder.

But the land was like a person to me, like many people, a family that was mine and that I had responsibility for. I remember my Papa tending to the animals and growing vegetables magically from the dirt where mud had been. I remembered my Mama tending the animals and working the land also. When she and Papa up and moved to the retirement home, it felt like it was my turn to hold things together.

I hadn't known my grandparents. They died before I was born. But Papa told me the stories of my German ancestors. They worked the land and replenished the livestock more than once when the herd of cows had been felled by disease. I was the first woman of my line to call herself a farmer. But there were plenty of women before me who worked the land. They just called themselves farmer's wives. That meant they cooked and cleaned and looked after their men and did farm chores too. It didn't seem fair to me – even if I was closer to Papa than Mama. When I inhaled near the pasture, I smelled more than cow dung. I smelled the musky scent of four generations of my family on the land.

So, after Papa died, I insisted that I could do it. I had Papa's memory to uphold. After he died, it was hard to bear all that grief. It felt like a skyscraper had collapsed onto me. I suspect being an only child made it harder. All the parent-child grief fell on one adult child: me. But I kept telling myself that Papa had secretly wanted the farm to continue. I could do that. It might have been silly for me to think that. Papa may have wanted the farm to continue. But what he really wanted was to not lose the farm and everything he had worked for. And I knew that what he told me was true. What he wanted most of all was for me to be happy.

I was happy being a *bucolicus*, a cowherder.

I didn't mind the mud. I didn't mind the dust. I didn't mind smelling like a cow when I went in my house (that my parents had once owned) and tracked in mud from the barn. This happened, no matter how hard I tried to clean my shoes. But I liked it. The dust combined with the musky scent reminded me of childhood. It reminded me of my Papa – minus the cigarette smoke. It reminded me of innocence and forever.

But my parents were right. It was hard financially. I barely made it. People began telling me the only way farmers could survive was by using the new machinery. I had to borrow money from Ainsley. I bought the machinery, only to find myself strapped again. The machinery just helped me stay afloat. I could pay the farmhands. I could pay my expenses, including taxes. But I had no extra cash to pay Ainsley back. Ainsley said it didn't matter. Ainsley was a lawyer with a firm in town and made plenty of money. But borrowing money – especially from Ainsley – mattered to *me*.

I almost didn't buy my leather purse. But it was marked down from the second-hand price at the local flea market. I've always thought that things happen for a reason. The twice marked down used leather purse was there and so was I. The money I had in my pocket was just enough. I looked up at the morning sky one more time – at the blue infused with yellow sun. The taffy-wisps of clouds had elongated. The sky-blue light was brighter. These small changes told me that time was passing. Then I looked down at the rolling pasture dotted with cows. It was all mine – for now.

I thanked God for the beautiful day – for the farm and for my memory of Papa. I thanked God for my life and for it all. Then I turned and walked down the side of the narrow road to the little church that was about a half mile away. Going to church made me feel stronger — and God knows I needed strength. I liked the little song that we sang each week – the song about how things were always the same and forever would be.

It comforted me and gave me the strength to go on – keeping things the same, or so I thought.

Chapter Five

Growing up, I would occasionally come to this church with Mama. Papa sometimes came along. Usually, he stayed home. "The newspaper is more interesting than the minister," is all he would say when Mama asked him to go to church. Eventually, I came to see that he was right, and I preferred to stay home and read the newspaper with Papa. After a while, Mama started staying home too. At first, she said the house should be clean for the Lord's Day. She often spent the morning cleaning – dusting the dark tan drapes and the rectangular teak coffee table. But after a few weeks of dusting furiously, she said she reckoned that the house was clean enough. Then she said that the Lord knew she meant to clean. She started sleeping in. I grew up thinking that Sunday was the Lord's Day to let your Mama rest while you and your Papa read the newspaper after the farm chores were done. I can't say we were a religious family.

The church had a new minister when I went back as an adult. He was a young handsome man who was smart too. I'm sure that's why many of the women were there – even the older ones. Probably more than a few of the men were there for the same reason. But who's to judge? I was glad the church was there. I enjoyed the singing – especially the Sundays the choir was there. I didn't know most of the songs. But once when a soloist sang and looked heavenward, it warmed my heart. On beautiful days like today, it was as if God rode on the rays of sun shining through the stained-glass windows. On dreary days, the church felt like a haven. It felt like the shelter that it was – but more so with all the people gathered.

My favorite service was Christmas Eve when light rippled from one white candle (candles were handed out to every person) to another. Before you knew it, the darkened sanctuary became bright. Maybe the light was a metaphor signifying the days would get longer again and that the sun would return. But to me the candlelight was just light—a rippling tradition – and I loved it.

Maybe it was all about the people. In truth, I rarely thought about the baby Jesus, or the Holy Ghost, or even the Holy Mother. I just liked being a part of something so much larger than me. Going to church was kind of like standing in a field and listening to the voice of God speaking through the beaks of shiny eyed crows, the long moos of cows, and the high-pitched whinnies of nearby horses. It was like breathing life into the stretched taffy clouds in the sky. It was like coming home and finding a hundred people cheering you on. *You can do it,* they would say in a collective voice, adding, *It's fate,* or *It's meant to be. Just put your mind to it. Or pray on it,* the older and more religious people couldn't help saying. Then we would eat together. It was called fellowship or breaking bread. People would bring their most yummy dishes to share after the service.

My stomach rumbled.

I guess it was the community that kept me coming. The food was part of the community.

I was surrounded by my neighbors and the church gave us something to talk about – even if it was only "wasn't that an inspiring sermon" or "I loved that song." That gave me a conversational opening to learn about my neighbors. I was relieved that I didn't have to talk about baking pies (it seemed I alone among the other farm women had no interest in it – even though I *do* like to eat pie!) and selling fruit and vegetables along the road in our farm stands. I did the latter, too, but how interesting is that for a conversational topic?

A woman farmer is unusual around these parts – maybe everywhere – and sometimes I felt the sting of rebuff. Just the other day at the vegetable stand, a customer asked me if I was a farmer's wife and I replied no and told her I was the farmer. I added that women can farm, too. So, I may have been a little defensive in my reply which never helps. At all costs, I didn't want to appear like a woman who was looking for a husband – for love or to increase my land holdings. I've heard of people getting married from different farms and ending up with twice the amount of land. It makes you wonder what the motivating factor is – love or greed? That was always my first thought. But my second thought was – and sometimes I had to remind myself – who am I to judge? I kept my opinions to myself.

The bottom line is that women are frequently competing over men, and I wanted no part of it. I had Ainsley, of course. But we kept a low-profile since we had an unconventional relationship. Also, I didn't want to spend time with the male farmers. It wasn't that I didn't like them. I just suspected we didn't have much in common. I had overheard a few conversations about who had the biggest tractor and the most advanced milking machine. I just wasn't that kind of farmer. I was content with what little I had.

I had faith that once my neighbors got to know me, they would warm up.

Usually, the sermons were pretty good. But today there was a guest minister speaking. His sermon lulled me to sleep a few times. Suddenly, I became aware of how uncomfortable the pew was. I guess that is what Ainsley doesn't like about going to church – you never knew what you were going to get.

The topic was why it is important for us to go to the memorial services of loved ones and friends. I agreed that it was important for us to give people a proper goodbye – even if they would be in our hearts forever, like the fresh air we breathed. But I couldn't help thinking that since most of the people who came to the church were over sixty (at least!) and there were more memorial services – that attendance (to both church and the memorial services) must be dropping off. As soon as I figured out that the guest minister (an older man who was a colleague of our younger minister who was away) had an agenda, I lost interest.

I probably would have fallen asleep longer instead of just nodding and jerking back awake, but Ainsley had made me an extra-strong cup of coffee (just the way I like it!) that morning before I left the house.

My mind started to wander when I noticed that the minister's robe was almost the same shade of brown as Cinnamon. I wondered if Cinnamon could come to church, would she? I imagined her walking down the aisle on her four legs and sitting up like a human in the pew. The pew would strain and creak under her. The people around her would hold up their hands to whisper as they made eye contact with each other. Some of them might stifle laughter. A few might even hold their noses in anticipation of the fact that she might have an "accident."

Poor Cinnamon, I thought.

It wasn't like she was purple. I mean she did fit in with the other cows. Besides, the sign outside the church said everyone was welcome. Didn't that mean cows were welcome also?

Who could deny she was a holy being? She had her own personality. Her own way of thinking and being. She was obviously intelligent (even if she thought I had no idea that she was spying on me). I strongly suspected she had emotions. She loved to run and play in the pasture, and she had special cow friends who I saw her with. The saying "sacred cow" didn't come out of nowhere.

My Bible knowledge has always been scant. But I do remember hearing something Biblical about animals being made to serve man. What about women – where did they come in? But I also heard the Bible said that cruelty against animals is a sin! That must be true. We had a beagle named Sparky when I was growing up, and I never ever thought of being cruel to him. I loved Sparky and let him jump up on me. Sometimes, he knocked me over. But I didn't care. I let him lick my face with his pink doggy tongue. In fact, when I heard there was such a thing as people being cruel to their pets (that's why the SPCA was created) I was incredulous and exclaimed, "People actually do that?!" I was still quite young and still remember the first feeling of being flushed with indignation.

Farm animals are animals too, just like my dog had been. It seemed like they would come under the Biblical definition of men having dominion over beasts – but they weren't really beasts. In my mind, beasts were scary and threatening. With the exception of the other day, when Cinnamon snorted at me for having a leather purse, I have never felt threatened by any of my farm animals. In fact, I have to stop myself from getting overly attached to them. The bleating sheep and the mewing baby lambs following them around are adorable, but I have always known –

since when I was young and was the one who used to feed them – that they would end up on someone's Easter table as the main course. But I was never able to eat them. When I once heard someone say that the Fatted Lamb was to die for, I thought she meant she had a heart condition. It turned out that she was talking about a restaurant.

It's sad, too, when the pigs are sold for slaughter. Baby pigs always make me think of baby humans. They are so pink and pretty. The last pig I sold was almost as long as a short adult and fetched a good price. God knows I needed the money. Thinking of God, reminded me I was in church. The guest minister was still droning on. *Was it a sin to sell a pig for slaughter if you needed the money? Maybe it was a sin to buy the pig for the smokehouse. What about the brick layer who helped to construct the smokehouse? Was it a sin if he was just doing his job? What if he was doing it to feed his family and his pet sheep dog who he considered to be part of the family? Was it a sin then? He would never think of eating his dog. Was there a difference between farm animals and domestic animals? They are both animals who live with humans and they both rely on humans for their food and shelter.*

I thought of the term, "thy daily bread." *Humans need shelter too and regular food. Were we really that different from animals, domestic or not?* I realized that I was making myself feel guilty. That made me feel angry. I wasn't that bad. I was just doing what my ancestors had done. And I have always tried not to sell off the male calves to the veal farms. We always did have to sell off the dairy cows when they were too old to give birth and produce milk, but I've always refused to think about what happens to them.

Whatever it was, something shifted. Suddenly, I could see things for what they were.

I shuddered. The graphic details of turning a calf into veal were so bad that when I first heard about this as a preteen, I refused to eat veal. I continued not to eat it. Maybe that was the beginning, or perhaps it was when I was a child and started being around the cows when I was doing chores. I would pet them after I fed them and tell them my secrets. I wanted to name them. But Mama warned me not to because they would be gone before I knew it. Now I could see that the farming machinery put distance between me and my old chores. It might have been the fact that the sheep and their nuzzling lambs looked so sweet together until they became … *you know*. Perhaps it was when I was a small child, and my mother counted my toes and recited the little piggy poem by Mother Goose.

One thing leads to another.

The minister said, "Amen." The shiny brass collection plates were passed. The clink of coins into them was a familiar sound. I felt reassured. I put in my envelope, smiled at the ushers, and stood with the others to sing the final hymn.

Then I went downstairs and stood near the food-laden table.

"Good afternoon, Jody," said a familiar looking woman, with curly brown hair and a round face, who greeted me. "What did you think of the sermon?"

Just in time, I popped a delicious meatball into my mouth.

I smiled and nodded as I chewed.

Chapter Six

"We're not that different than her," I murmured. I knew this from my spying.

It didn't seem like my friend was buying it.

My friend looked at me with her big brown eyes. Then she rolled them.

I was talking to the cow who I'm closest too. We were born around the same time. I felt her tail flicking my side.

We loved each other. But suddenly, there was a divide cause by our different opinions.

"Not different? What in God's green pasture do you mean?" asked my friend.

"'God's green pasture'? What are you talking about?" I responded.

"It was just something I heard our captor say. I have no idea what she meant. Everyone knows the pasture is part of the universe. Maybe 'God' means universe." When my friend finished talking, she lowered her head and sniffed the grass.

I moved my shoulders and shrugged while I stood and looked out over the rolling pasture. I wondered if the fence in front of the line of leafy green trees had any openings in it.

"Everyone has a different way of saying the same thing," I replied.

"I thought you were saying we're not that different from our captor," my friend replied.

Apparently, she had decided not to munch on the grass. She stood before me with her head raised and her mouth full of nothing but words.

I put my head down and nibbled on a blade of grass. I had no intention of getting caught up in wordplay. But suddenly I didn't like the word "captor."

Mid-blade, I stopped chewing and put my head back up and looked at my friend seriously.

"Please don't call her our 'captor'," I said. "That's not useful to us."

"Why? I've heard you refer to her as our 'captor.'"

"That's different. I changed my mind. Captors are like cowboys with lassos at rodeos. They are people who torture other animals – animals like…" – I had to think hard – "… like lions and elephants in the circus when it comes through town. We see the big circus trucks going by on the highway. We hear the humans talking about them. The animals are captured and then put on display. People keep them at bay with big whips. By comparison, we are not captured."

"No, we are just led to a fenced-in field with the promise of food and water. Then we are led into that stinky barn with the same promises," my friend answered.

I stood mutely, unable to argue with her.

She was unable to help adding: "See I'm right."

"Ok. Ok," I assented. "You have a point. We're not here of our free will. But we've rarely tried to run away. When we do, it doesn't work. You don't hear about cows escaping from farms and living peacefully in the woods."

My friend nodded.

"Anything could happen to us out there," she replied thoughtfully. Then she chewed her cud.

"Exactly," I said, relieved that we finally found something we could agree on. Before my friend could walk away, I quickly added, "That's why it's to our advantage that we have lots in common with the captor, I mean our human companion."

My friend widened her big brown eyes at me until she elongated the dark brown spots on her face.

"Companion?!"

"Yes, companion," I replied seriously. "We are companions and have things in common."

"Such as?"

"For one thing, we breathe the same air."

My friend nodded and said, "and?"

"We both need to eat," I added, swatting a fly from my side.

"That's true," said my friend in a rather prissy way. I had never seen this behavior coming from her before.

I imagined she just didn't like the fact I was right. She was standing more erect, and her words were crisp.

"And if she eats, she must shi—"

I said this because I wanted my friend to be less tense, but she interrupted me and said:

"Defecate," said my friend, wording it more properly. Then she asked, "Have you seen her defecate?"

The fact was I hadn't seen the nice human defecate, but I knew humans did eliminate. Once, I saw one of the farmhands who was working in the pasture pulling down his fly (I wondered why they call it that – I think of a fly as something to swat away) to urinate. He turned his back to me when he saw me staring. But he didn't have anything, I hadn't seen before – even if it was on a bull and bigger. This was the same man who had put his arm up my you know what to inseminate me, so I guess someone might say he was being a gentleman to turn his back. Though, I think there's a chance he was embarrassed.

"Well," I replied slowly. I wasn't ready to admit there might be a gap in my argument. "She may not have as many stomachs as us, so she doesn't go as often as we do. But I've seen her disappear at times especially when I was spying on her in the morning, so she may have some special place that she goes to relieve herself."

"Hmmm. So…you haven't seen her defecating. That means that you really don't know," said my friend. She was less erect and breathing normally. She had a gleam in her eye that faced me as she stared straight ahead through the wooden fence. She looked like she felt like she could relax now that she was right again.

"I've seen her eat," I replied stubbornly (refusing to admit defeat), "and it has to go somewhere."

"Wait a minute," said my friend. "I've seen her eating the products that our milk becomes, such as chocolate ice cream cones and thick and gooey grilled cheese sandwiches. At least I think milk becomes ice cream unless ice cream comes straight out of us."

"That's beside the point," I countered. I wasn't even going to try to explain that drippy chocolate ice cream cones didn't come straight out of our udders.

My friend looked at me triumphantly as if this was the end of our conversation and she had won.

"What I started out to say," I stated authoritatively, "is that we breathe the same air as her and we have the same emotions."

"Wait a minute," snorted my friend. "There's no way the human whatever could know what it feels like to constantly be kept pregnant and then to have your babies taken away. Then on top of that, we suffer the indignation of the milking machines. She may be nice to us but only because we give her what she wants. And after we're done making babies and producing milk, we get sent away and then are killed…"

I glared at her. She glared back. The air between us tightened. The sun might still be shining and the sky clear blue, but it couldn't be any more electrified than if the dark gray clouds of a bad thunder and lightning storm moved in. She had brought up the unspeakable. We both knew what happened when we stopped being able to give birth and produce milk. After we were used up, we were sent away. Most of us suspected the same fate was waiting for us that befell our male calves. I had refused to repeat what I heard in the barn that day not so long ago when the older cow was giving the younger one advice. I kept the terror away from me, by thinking that whoever ended up eating our old (and probably diseased) flesh, deserved whatever was coming. Plus, the future seemed like a long way off. Still, it was ominous.

We didn't speak for a few minutes.

I turned away from her and lowered my head to the ground where I pretended to chew on some grass. I had lost my appetite. I hoped I had turned away soon enough so that she didn't see the big tears that welled up in my eyes.

I took a breath and let the tears recede. Then I started to eat the grass for real, even though I wasn't hungry. I found a patch where the blades of grass were as sweet as the hay they put out for us.

My feelings were still hurt so I kept my head down.

Eating made me feel better.

"Look, there's the human you were talking about," observed the other cow. I no longer thought of her as my friend. I didn't intend to stand close to her anymore.

"Watch," I said, careful not to look at my former friend. "You'll see that I'm right. She has the same emotions that we do.

And we don't know what she's been through. She's going to let me out of the pasture. You'll see."

"Right," snarled the other cow sarcastically.

"You bet I'm right," I countered. "I know because I'm so special that she named me. My name is Cinnamon."

"Cinnamon! It sounds like she thinks you are something for sale at a strip mall."

Hmmm. This other cow must have been paying attention to some of the humans who came to stand on the other side of the wooden fence to visit us.

I pointedly ignored her comment and walked over to the wooden gate with the "X" in the middle of it. The "X" was made from thick wire.

"Cinnamon!" exclaimed my new human friend, the farmer, as she petted my nose that jutted out from the fence. "I'm sorry, baby. I didn't bring anything special home for you."

"I bet she was stuffing her own face, wherever she was," grumbled the other cow under a low moo.

I pointedly ignored her comment.

I looked up beseechingly at the human.

"Cinnamon, what are you trying to tell me? Look at you sticking your nose through the wire guards on the gate. You look like you are in a cage, and that's not right."

I squeezed my eyes shut and thought hard. I spelled the word "O-P-E-N" with my mind. I imagined the wispy clouds in the sky were rearranging themselves into my thoughts –

"O-P-E-N."

I kept my eyes shut and concentrated on the fact that my human companion could get the message and do what I wanted.

I looked up at her with my big brown eyes and pleaded. I saw that she was looking up at the sky. She started talking like someone was up there:

"Does this make up for selling off the pig for slaughter – even though I needed the money? It may be that comes under the mistreatment of animals. And maybe that is a sin. I hope you can forgive me. Perhaps you can forgive me because in this moment I am doing the right thing and letting your creature roam free."

We weren't anywhere near the wire where the birds liked to perch like clothespins on a clothesline. There weren't any trees nearby that were home to birds and squirrels. I had no idea who she was talking to, but I noticed that her hand was on the latch. She was letting me out!

I kept my head lowered. I didn't want to let on with my eyes that I thought she was crazy for talking to the sky. When she opened the gate, I walked right through it like I had never doubted she would do as I wished. I listened with no small amount of satisfaction as she latched the gate behind me.

"See," I couldn't help saying as I quickly turned my head over my shoulder as we passed that cow who was still on the OTHER side of the fence. Who was right now?

"You'll be back by milking time," she sneered in a low tone.

Maybe that was true, but meanwhile I was free. Plus, I had learned a new word: sin. Thinking about sin helped my human friend understand what I wanted and unlatch the gate. But I had never heard the word before. What was "sin" anyway?

Chapter Seven

That week on Thursday morning, like I did every Thursday, I went to visit Mama in her retirement home on the outskirts of town. I took the old silver pickup that had a few bales of hay in the open cargo area in the back behind the cab. I rolled down the window, looked up, and searched the sky. The weather people on the radio and the television were rarely right about the weather anymore so I made my own predictions. There was a puffy gray nimbus cloud to the right, and I wondered how long it would be before we had rain. I tried to figure out which direction the wind was moving. I licked my left finger but didn't feel anything.

I had an irrigation system installed for the crops, so it didn't matter if it rained or not because they would still get water. If it did rain, the hay in the back of the truck would get wet. But I still wished for rain. The floppy green leaves of the sunflowers looked like they were reaching for the sun. This was my favorite time of year – just before the sunflowers started to bloom. Vibrations from the colors of green soon to become yellow filled the air. The yellow petals may be microscopic right now but soon they would grow to their full size and be as bright as the sun.

Some of the green leaves stemming from the thick green stalk were starting to look wilted. I hoped their leaves and roots would soon be wet with rain. If it didn't rain, I would have to water the plants around the house where there was no irrigation system. It was more than the fact I didn't want to water the plants. I didn't feel like it. This feeling was new to me. Usually, I went right outside and filled my watering can with the hose attached to the side of the house. I never stopped to think of whether I felt like it or not. It was as if my purpose was to keep the plants alive. The oppressive heat may have had something to do with my mood. All I wanted to do was to stay cool. But I wanted to eat too. The heat made me extra hungry.

The air was still. There wasn't even a tiny breeze, the kind that makes it easier to breathe on a hot summer day. It seemed like the earth needed water. It looked parched and it felt worse. I could feel the dry cracks when I had been walking to the pickup. You can never have enough water. As a planter, I know that's not always true. But that's how it felt at that exact moment.

I put the keys in the ignition, started the pickup and pulled out of the front gate. Gravel crunched under the tires. Then I stopped again. Leaving the keys hanging from the ignition, I jumped out of the truck – okay, I should say I gingerly got out of the truck. I used to jump, but I'd been gaining weight and my knees had started to hurt, so I stared being more cautious. Then I latched and locked the gate behind me and got back into the cab. I looked at the sky one more time and whispered "PLEASE." It was my way of uttering a mini prayer. Then I pulled out onto the lonely two-lane highway. I arrived at my mother's retirement home in no time.

At the home, we had lunch in the dining room. I chose the *cordon bleu* chicken which tasted like it was baked with white wine. Mama had the same and remarked that the ham and cheese inside made it particularly tasty. I thought of the pig that I had sold briefly but the image of it floated away. I had needed the money. Plus, who was I to raise a ruckus – or even to comment on a single piece of ham. I could still taste my usual bacon I had for breakfast.

We practically ignored the overcooked stalks of broccoli and carrot slices next to the *cordon bleu* chicken. But we dutifully cleaned our plates.

"My compliments to the chef," I told the waitress, a middle-aged doughy woman. I guessed she was supplementing her farm's income.

I asked her if it was cooked in the French style.

"We wouldn't cook it any other way. It's baked in white wine and that's Swiss cheese melted on the top – though you can't see the holes."

She beamed at me.

I smiled back. Then I turned to my mother and asked her how her week was. She said that another friend of hers had passed and she needed to buy a third black dress. She explained that she only had two. She didn't want to risk being seen wearing the same one to another funeral.

"Goodness!" I exclaimed, patting my mouth with my linen napkin. The waitress was striding toward us with an ear-to-ear grin on her face.

She was carrying our desert – two chocolate puddings – with dollops of whipped cream on top.

I was trying to cut back, but goodness knows I couldn't ask the waitress to take it back. She would be insulted. I had known pudding was coming for dessert, but I didn't know it would be piled high with whipped cream.

I looked around. We were in a home-style dining room complete with lace tablecloths and sheer drawn-back curtains. The windows looked out into a trimmed yard that had a forest behind it. It was homey enough here for me to feel like I was a guest in someone's dining room. I wouldn't think of sending back food. It would be like insulting the host. Besides, the waitress was on the chubby side. She might take it personally if I told her I was trying to cut back.

"Mmm. Mmm," I said, smiling as I ate.

I was trying to cheer Mama up. I imagined her comforting me when I was a toddler and had a scraped knee. She always gave me chocolate ice cream. I had loved chocolate ice cream, and she would give me several scoops to make me feel better. Come to think of it, I don't remember if the injury or the ice cream came first. Maybe my love of chocolate ice cream came from my love of my Mama trying to cheer me up with it. I tried not to hear my thoughts as a voice in my head said, *Perhaps I injured myself just to get the ice cream.*

Mama licked the last bit off the spoon.

"They *do* have good pudding here," she commented.

I smiled at her. My strategy seemed to be working.

"I think it's the old-fashioned kind of pudding they have to cook," she added, "rather than the new pudding you just stir into milk before refrigerating it."

"I wasn't aware that there was a difference," I murmured. I felt self-conscious because Mama might pick up on the fact I didn't even know how to make pudding.

"The whipped cream was divine," I said.

I realized later I didn't even know where it came from – a can, a plastic bowl? Was the whipped cream homemade also? It was cream so I guess it originally came from a cow. I really had no idea. But I sensed that knowing where the food came from would somehow make it less magical. So, instead I said, "It was so good, so light and fluffy like clouds but heavenly. It was like eating the wings of angels."

Mama snapped out of her pudding-induced coma.

"It sounds like you've been going to church," she deduced as she narrowed her eyes.

"How's that been working for you?"

"Just fine," I replied. Mama was suspicious of church folks as being hypocrites. The wives would put on their Sunday finest and not admit their lives weren't perfect (by any means) and then they would gossip about each other. Whenever she heard someone being particularly nasty, Mama would comment later that the woman's husband probably beat her and since she couldn't confront him, she was mean to another woman who didn't deserve it. I always agreed with Mama and, rightly or wrongly, grew up thinking there was lots of unspoken suffering among farm folks.

We decided to sit outside after lunch. Mama said she needed a change of pace. I offered to take her dress shopping, but she replied she preferred to shop alone, and she could take the senior bus to the shopping mall the next day. I breathed a sigh of relief I hoped wasn't too evident. I really didn't care for shopping, and I detested going to dress shops where the sizes were always too small for me. Mama was several sizes smaller than the largest sizes most dress shops carried. They might eat well at the home, but she went to her senior fitness group three times a week.

We went out the front door and followed the pavement. It was still clear – not a drop of rain in sight. I scanned the sky. The large rain cloud I had seen earlier appeared to have blown away. I could no longer see it. But I wasn't a sunflower reaching for sun. I was searching for shade. Just as my knees began to hurt, I spotted a shady pavilion with an empty bench under it.

"I already miss Edna. She's my third friend to die in three months," said Mama.

I was figuring out how to change the subject, which turned out not to be so easy without the enticement of chocolate pudding topped with whipped cream. I looked up at the clear blue bell of the sky again.

"I saw a rain cloud, before I left the farm. But it appears to have gone away," I said and added, "I was hoping it would rain – for the flowers."

Mama nodded but wasn't taking the bait to change the subject.

"I used to sit next to Edna every morning and have breakfast with her," she reminisced.

"What did she like to eat?" I thought we might detour into talking about food.

"Oh, Edna loved her bacon."

"Mmm," I replied. "Bacon. I love it too. Nice and crispy and delicious."

"That's probably why she fell over dead," said Mama.

She seemed to be oblivious to my comment – or not. I noticed her eying my mid-section. Suddenly, I was self-conscious. My belly was bigger than usual and strained the white plastic flower buttons on my favorite pale pink cotton blouse.

"I tried to get Edna to eat oatmeal with me, but no. She just screwed up her face and announced that she never could stand the stuff. "Too pasty," she would say. Whatever that meant. Then she would order her usual bacon and eggs. I have that occasionally, too. But I have oatmeal on most days."

"At least she knew what she liked," I said, attempting to be cheerful.

"Yes. And because she refused to change, she's dead," said Mama sadly.

I didn't know what to say. As it turned out, I didn't have to say anything.

Mama wasn't done talking.

"Jody, I've been meaning to talk to you. I've noticed that you've put on a lot of weight in the past year since you replaced manual labor with the farm machines. I suspect that the machines are saving you a lot of work but that you are getting less exercise. Maybe you should take a walk a few times a week and cut back on whatever it is that you are eating."

I used to walk years ago when I was in the local college. I was majoring in finance and thought I would get a job in accounting like Papa. He was able to make a good salary and support the farm. I had stopped walking in my first year. In my second year, I had gained so much weight that my clothes no longer fit me. After two years, I couldn't lie to myself anymore. I hated college and I hated majoring in finance. I was going to take some time off and figure out what I wanted to do so I went home and never left. That's how I became a farmer. I loved it at first and after a few months of doing chores, I had lost the excess weight I had gained in college. Now here I was again. I had to admit to myself that I was unhappy. But I couldn't admit that to Mama.

I was going to tell Mama that I did walk to church almost every week, but she wasn't done talking.

"Your father didn't like to talk about his background, and we didn't want to scare you. But I do remember telling you at least once about your uncle who died when you were little. He leaned over to pick up something from the ground, and just like that he fell over dead. He was still a young man, and he had small children." Mama wiped a tear from her eye.

That tear jolted me into reality. She wasn't just criticizing me about my weight. Grief had broken her in two and opened her up. She went from mourning her friend to thinking about me, her only child. She had lost my father, who was her friend as well as her spouse. They did things together. They went to the movies. They took walks – even if Papa was chain smoking with every step. He was also her best friend. She was alone in the world, save for her friends that she saw every day and except for her only child, me, who called most days and usually visited once a week. She wasn't being critical. She cared about me.

"Remember your Papa's parents died in their early forties, just before you were born. They both had heart problems."

She looked at me expectantly.

"Don't worry Mama, I'll try to do better."

I was reassuring my Mama that she wouldn't lose me too. I meant what I said. I didn't want to let her down.

Chapter Eight

Sometimes change takes a long time. Like standing in the pasture for what seems like an eternity. Or like being herded to the barn three times a day for milking times – which is so tedious it feels endless. Once I'm hooked up to the milking machine, it seems like it's yanking at me forever. But I know that's not true. Because when I'm done, I go back in the pasture again, along with the others. And the pasture is a big improvement over the barn.

Today I snuck out of the pasture by going to the very back, down the hill and up another hill, to where the tree line is. Following the fence, I found a place where the ground was uneven. I kept on walking and found an opening in the fence big enough for me to get through. I thought there might be one. Probably, it happened like I imagined it did. One of the farmhands – most likely the surly one – would have stopped to wipe his brow with his red kerchief. He would've looked around and if the coast was clear, he might have taken out the ham sandwich that he kept in the front pocket of his overalls. Then he would stand there and unwrap it. By the time that he finished eating it, he would've forgotten where he left off building the fence and started again, leaving an opening. Or he may have realized there was a gap, but he didn't care. It was less work for him and what did he care if some cows got lost. We weren't *his* cows. We knew that – even if we assumed we were our own animals. Everyone knew the nice farmer woman hired the farmhands and didn't pay attention to the fact one of them didn't seem to like taking orders from a woman. Of course, this is what I imagined. But I do know for a fact that one of the farmhands – the one who is big enough so that he looks like *he* should have an udder – carries a ham sandwich in the front pocket of his denim overalls. I've seen him eat it. Once when he spied me watching him, he told me that he would give me some, but it might make me sick, and he didn't want to risk that. As it turned out, the sandwich did make me feel sick, but that was when I sniffed the air and smelled the tang of ham. It probably wasn't my friend from the pen because this was before he was sold off. But just the idea of someone eating another creature made me nauseas. What if someone made a sandwich out of the farmhand? As much as I distrusted him, I wouldn't have wanted to see that.

I went through the opening. Going through that gap made it feel like a huge weight was lifted from me. I was free! Then I remembered I had a plan to come back to the pasture – eventually. Still, I was momentarily free! I was choosing to do what I wanted, instead of obeying someone else. I stayed next to the fenced-in pasture on the outside of the fence. The land was so different that it was a little scary. For one thing, the forest was dark. The tall trees got in the way of the sun. I started to hear noises. After my eyes adjusted to the darkness, I saw a family nestled further away from the fence. The largest one had horns looking like sturdy young tree branches. A slender one without horns suckled the young ones. I deduced the one with the horns must be the father and the one doing the suckling was probably the mother.

So, these were the creatures that lived in the wild – the famous wild deer with their spotted fawns. They didn't seem that scary. They seemed docile, content to live their own lives. It seemed like they were oblivious to me. But then I stepped on a big stick that made a crackling noise. The family started, as if they were used to things making them run away, but then the mother and the father widened their eyes and stayed put as if seeing me was incredulous.

"Just passing by," I said to reassure them. Then I kept on going, making sure I was near the pasture fence. I kept up a good pace. I had places to go. Somehow, I lost sight of the fence. Eventually I came to a road I hadn't seen before. The road was made of yellow mud. The tire tracks were so deep that squirrels could hide in them. It looked like the tread was left by a tractor. Fortunately, there weren't any vehicles on the road, just me, walking briskly along. I swished my tail behind me and pretended I knew where I was going.

I sensed I was going in the right direction. Then I saw a pale golden rump with a long smooth white tale hanging straight down. The rump was next to another rump with another lengthy tail. I recognized where I was. I had heard the farmhands talking about the horse farm next door. From the pasture, the horses were just small dots. It wasn't worth it to me to even try to move closer to see them. Horses, horses, horses. It was all that the farmhand, the one I didn't care for, got excited about. He wished he worked for the horse farm. Blah, blah, blah. Well so did I. That way I wouldn't have to see him.

The horses were outside of their brick stable to the far left of the cow pasture. Fortunately, the horses' behinds were facing me and not their heads. They wouldn't see me as I walked by. Since I was on the other side of the fence (and not in the cow pasture where I usually was), who knew what they would think if they saw me. They might have reared and whinnied in fright thinking that I was a wild beast coming out of the woods. Maybe they would have mistaken me for a deer. They may not have recognized me since I wasn't where they usually saw me. Horses are not nearly as intelligent as people give them credit for.

I went to the end of the road and couldn't believe what I saw. Metal contraptions – large cars, driven by humans – rushed by on a paved highway. They were going so fast that I don't think they saw me. Somehow, I had escaped not only the fenced-in pasture but the outer gate as well. This must be the same road the young cows ran down when they escaped. Suddenly, I had a plan.

CINNAMON: A dairy cow's (and her farmer's) path to freedom

I was relieved to see the fence again. I could feel its woody roughness rubbing my side as I walked beside it. The fence wasn't getting away from me again. If it weren't for the electric wire just above the wooden fence, I could have flattened the fence and barged back into the pasture. But I didn't want to go back there yet. It was close to milking time, and I was sick of going back and forth from the pasture to the barn. Back and forth, back and forth. The pasture. The barn. And then again. How boring! There were so many cows the farm hands wouldn't miss just one. Even if a farmhand did notice my stall was empty when he hooked the machines up, he probably wouldn't care.

I continued to walk so close to the fence I could feel my side brushing the coarse wood. The people in the cars whizzing by probably wouldn't even see me walking under the trees. They probably were looking at the road in front of them and if they turned, they would see what they expected to see: cows in a pasture, placidly chewing our cuds. They wouldn't expect to see one on the outside of the fence. If some drivers were unusually observant, they would think they were seeing things. "Look," one human would say to another, "that cow looks like she wants to come with us to the mall." The other one would laugh. I had it all figured out.

I kept walking and spotted a short yellow forklift parked in front of the main gate. I smiled to myself. This was the vehicle the farmhand who travelled with a ham sandwich in his front pocket liked to drive. If he was the one working today, I was in luck. I suspected that he rarely saw anything outside of himself – except for his ham sandwiches. I stopped in my tracks because I saw a succulent weed in front of me. Now that my plan was in place, I could stop, relax, and enjoy myself. I could even have a little snack!

Presently, the mean but oblivious farmhand who I hoped was working today pulled his old dirty white pickup in front of the gate. Then he got out, walked over to the outside gate, and unlocked and unlatched it. Then he got in the dirt-splattered yellow forklift. From my new hiding spot behind a stand of trees, I followed him into the farm outside of the pasture – to where the farmhouse was. He drove the forklift over the cinders of the driveway. That fast, I was right behind him. I didn't even look at the rolling pasture which I knew was right in front of me, through the second gate. I just scooted to the left and hid behind another group of trees. I watched as the forklift idled. The farmhand looked like he was eating something – maybe it was the ham sandwich he usually carried. I waited until he went around the corner into the barn and then I walked in the direction of the farmhouse.

It was still morning. Streaks of sunrise colored the sky. I was surprised that it wasn't later – at least noon or later in the afternoon. I guess my adventure really didn't take that long. My plan was to find out more about my human friend. I snuck up to the farmhouse and peeked in the window. The room was empty. I was disappointed. I had hoped to watch my human friend eating her breakfast and to see if she had changed anything, since she had read my thoughts, and opened the gate the other day.

I lowered my head and smelled another white daisy. I didn't see it the last time that I was here, so it must have just bloomed recently. Chomp. It was gone. I said I was going to cut back but that didn't include white daisies or yellow ones if I saw them. Daisies were a delicacy! I wondered if my human friend had any delicacies that she liked to eat. For some reason, I thought of sunflowers.

I had no interest in eating sunflowers. For starters, they were too tall to reach without considerable effort. I could chomp at the stalks and knock them down. But that seemed like too much work. The stalks were thick and green and chewier looking than anything I cared to eat. Also, the large petals of the flowers didn't look that succulent to me. By comparison the daisy petals looked tender. And they were tasty!

Plus, there were the birds. I would have to compete with them. The yellow finches were always around the sunflowers. At first, I thought they must like the seeds like the other birds. I assumed they were drawn to the color yellow because they were bright yellow too. But then I saw a yellow finch devouring the wide green leaves before they grew into flowers. The finch was going after the young sunflower plant (which had yet to flower) with such ferocity that it looked like she wanted to be the most yellow thing around – and she was going to start by decimating the sunflowers before they had seeds or petals.

A sunflower that survived was so elegant standing there reaching for the sun and at the same time drooping its seed-heavy head as it ripened into itself. Suddenly, it occurred to me that if I was going to name my human farmer friend, I would call her Sunflower. She was big and sunny with shaggy golden curls and here she was on a farm where animals were sold off to be slaughtered (really, there's no other way to describe it) and she had a good word for everyone. She loved to eat and was frequently seen walking around with a chocolate ice cream cone. Her love of food was like a sunflower soaking in the sun.

It occurred to me that "Sunflower" might be my private name for the farmer woman, but she could never understand the name because she couldn't understand me when I spoke to her. Thinking of her, I raised my head and looked back into the window and caught a glimpse of Sunflower sitting at the table.

She was holding up a pink piece of flesh on her fork and smelling it. She sniffed it and said something to the person standing behind her at the stove. For a minute, I forgot about what she was eating and watched as she spoke to the person behind her. Never before had I wanted to be a human. I had never even thought about it. But at that instant I wished I could be someone who Sunflower could talk to so easily. She turned back and gingerly sniffed the pink piece of flesh on her fork. It looked like what was called bacon, but I couldn't smell anything. Then she put the flesh in her mouth and chewed. I assumed the windows were tighter that morning, and the stench of the cooked pig flesh couldn't reach me.

The orange house cat appeared in the empty chair at the end of the table. He leaned his furry triangular face over the table and looked at the farmer expectantly. The farmer held a piece of pink flesh out to the cat. The cat sniffed and then turned away, putting its orange tail where it's face had been. The cat curled up in a ball on the chair. It looked like nap time.

I wondered what this meant. The farmer might be eating something different. But, then again, it wouldn't be the first time a cat turned up his nose at food he normally liked.

I lowered my head again and began to sniff around for something tasty to eat. I assumed the window was tighter, and that Sunflower hadn't changed at all. Did the fact she could read my thoughts, spelled out by the clouds above me, mean nothing to her?

She was still eating my friends.

I sighed. I felt a lump in my throat and salty tears nipping at my eyes, so I nibbled on the purple violets growing next to the house. Food always made me feel so much better. Then I heard the front door open and close.

The voice of my friend Sunflower said, "Cinnamon! You clever girl. You've been out here spying on me! Ainsley was right."

Ainsley!? Who was Ainsley?

Then I remembered. Ainsley must be the person who stood at the stove behind Sunflower.

I let Sunflower scratch my ears as she steered me back toward the pasture. It felt so good that momentarily I didn't mind going back to the pasture even though I knew the farmhand could find me there.

"How did you get out of the pasture, Cinnamon?" she asked – as if I would tell her even if I could.

I looked up at her with my big brown eyes and gave her my blankest look.

"Someone must have left the gate open," she said as she unlatched the gate and let me back in.

You have no idea, I thought.

Chapter Nine

"I've long known animal products aren't good for me, but it's the suffering of the animals that did it. I couldn't bear knowing the food I'm paying for was going to an industry that is profiting from the suffering of animals. I know it's hard, but it is possible not to eat meat. This dish looks just as tasty without the bacon that I had the waiter withhold." Candace paused and ate some of her clam's casino appetizer.

I was silent as I studied the menu. I had been talking to a grain hybrid distributor about some improvements in the seeds and arrived around twenty minutes late. My friend had been understanding. But now I had to order my food in front of her.

What could I order that wouldn't offend my friend? We were in the restaurant of her choice, the fanciest eating establishment in town. When she asked me to dinner and I balked because I know she has expensive tastes, Candace sensed how I was feeling and generously offered to pay.

I told her we could eat somewhere less expensive, but she didn't like any of my suggestions.

"I'm sorry...," she continued. "I shouldn't be talking about people who make a living off the suffering of animals. I know you're a farmer."

"A dairy farmer," I reminded her. "The cows that live on my farm make milk, which is natural for them."

I didn't tell her about the male calves who were sold off to be raised as beef, or worse, to be killed when they were still young so they could be turned into veal. I didn't mention that the female cows were sold off to slaughterhouses after three or four breeding and milking cycles. Since I tried not to think about that myself, I wasn't about to say it out loud. I didn't dare divulge that the lambs we raised became Easter dinner. And I didn't mention I had to sell the hog to pay for the taxes on the farm.

I didn't tell her any of this because she might cause a scene right here in her favorite restaurant. I also didn't want to make her feel sick. But I admit that a larger part of me didn't want to have to deal with Candace making a scene in public. I had known Candace for a long time and well enough to imagine that she would throw a fit in public without thinking twice. I had seen her slamming down her silverware and storming out. I had heard her raising her voice. I knew she was capable of it.

I avoid conflict at all costs because I have always hated it. It wasn't that I would have to come back to the restaurant and be embarrassed about Candace's behavior. The last time I had come to this restaurant was almost a year ago because Candace had insisted on coming here then too.

I lowered my eyes, picked up the leather-bound rectangular menu, opened it, and studied it like my life depended on me choosing the right thing. It might be Candace's favorite place, but they did have beef on the menu. This was farming country after all, and it seemed like very few people had any compunctions about eating meat. I noticed they served veal. It was called veal Marsala and was billed as being delicious and tender and was complete with sautéed mushrooms and wine. It reminded me of calves with spindly little legs. I'd sold more than a few of the male calves off to the veal farms when I was desperate for money. (The veal farms paid more per pound than the beef farms did.) But selling calves to the veal farms left a bad taste in my mouth and I tried to avoid it. If I was going to run a conventional dairy farm, I couldn't help having to sell off the male calves that were born. But it made me more aware about where beef and veal came from and what the differences were.

When I look back, I see that I knew it was cruel to eat beef, but I resigned myself to the fact that cruelty is part of life. But even when I was still eating beef, I refused to eat veal. I knew how the calves were starved to become tender and I found it so distasteful that even the thought of eating veal made me feel sick. So, I wasn't going to order veal Marsala, although I do love almost anything cooked in red wine.

Fortunately, the restaurant was surf and turf, and the menu had a seafood section. I was still deciding but I had it narrowed down between the scallops and the rainbow trout wrapped in parchment.

"It's only natural for cows to give milk to their calves when they are suckling. It's NOT natural for them to provide milk for humans. I once heard a woman doctor say, that 'the only babies that should be drinking cow milk are baby cows,'" commented Candace.

"That may be so," I countered. But the fact is that the cows wouldn't be here if they weren't providing milk. They are born to grow up and be milked. People drink milk and eat cheese," I said, thinking *not to mention the butter that's in your clams casino*.

"It's still suffering," maintained Candace. "If they are just born because they can provide milk – at least the half of them that are born female – then they're living totally artificial lives, lives that exist to accommodate humans."

"That may be so, but it doesn't change the fact people still want to drink milk and eat cheese. It doesn't change the fact that dairy farmers have to make a living," I adamantly replied.

I was surprised at the level of defensiveness I felt rising in me. I was usually more even keel, but Candace had struck a nerve by saying I was making a living off animal suffering. I wanted to hurt her back. I knew she felt inadequate because she had never had to work. She confided this in me once and I never forgot it. So, it didn't surprise me when she flinched when I said dairy farmers had to make a living. I didn't feel bad that I had to make a living. Almost everybody did. I was one of the lucky ones without a mortgage. That meant other farmers were really struggling.

Candace regarded me silently for a moment.

"People who eat meat are often aggressive," she stated, breaking the silence. "They pick up the aggressiveness from the animals they ingest. The animal knows it's going to be slaughtered. Think about it. A cow or steer who is forced to walk down the chute must know it's going to be killed and this produces adrenaline in the animal. Then people eat that adrenaline in their steaks and hamburgers."

I had just stopped eating red meat recently – after I talked to Mama about being more conscious about my health. But I had eaten lots of beef in my life. The meatball at church had been my last bit. After I stopped eating red meat, I began to feel more attuned to the emotions of cows. I could swear that Cinnamon was trying to talk to me. But I couldn't tell Candace that and run the risk that she would think I was crazy.

Given that I had eaten so much beef over the years, there must be a residue of adrenaline left in my body. After I stopped eating beef, it began to smell bad to me. It *was* dead flesh. But maybe there was more to the rotten smell.

Suddenly, I felt nauseous. I tried to be more rational. It made sense that growing up on a farm, I would've been taught eating meat was the most wholesome and natural thing in the world. Husbanding animals was how my parents had provided for our lives. It was all I knew and since my parents' parents were also farmers, it was all they had known.

Rumor had it that Candace lived off a trust fund left to her by wealthy parents who died when she was still a child. Candace and I became friends in second grade, a year after her parents died in a car accident. She was raised by her grandparents who moved to the area. Her grandfather did something with finances and her grandmother was what used to be called a society lady. Her grandmother hired a succession of nannies to take care of Candace. Once, Candace had confided in me (when we were still in elementary school) that when she would get attached to a nanny, her grandmother (who never spoke about her mother or the fact that she had died) would fire the nanny, and a new one was hired.

I was still Candace's friend (others had dropped away) because I knew she was a good person. She was just wounded. Now and then (it got worse as she got older), she tried to wound someone back – or wound them first. It was, after all, what had happened to her. That's what she expected out of life. So, her behavior made sense to me. Tonight, she was at her worst. I wondered why she was acting the way she did. Was it the anniversary of her parents' death? Or did something happen to remind her of that day? Or was it something else?

I took a breath and thought of all the years we had been friends. I thought of all the times she had been there for me. I thought of the way in which we contained each other as friends. We knew each other's history and we also had a shared history. I took another breath and felt my defensiveness float away. I had a change of heart. My inner voice said I could confide in her.

"Everybody suffers," I said gently. "But I do understand what you are talking about with the suffering of animals. About three months ago, I felt upset by the fact that I had to sell our biggest hog to pay the taxes on the farm," I said, pausing. "I always loved the book, *Charlotte's Web*. Maybe that's why I got so upset when we had to sell the hog. In my childhood imagination, pigs had feelings and spiders wrote messages in their webs. But that book was about one pig on one farm. There are so many pigs on so many farms – even if there are fewer farms than there used to be.

"Pigs are known for being very intelligent," I continued. "But after I sold the hog, I kept eating bacon because I loved bacon and that's what I did each morning. I was used to it, and I loved the taste. But then I saw Mama. She's been going to so many funerals of her friends and she talked to me because she was concerned about me gaining weight." I paused. Had Candace noticed too? She made no indication she had noticed and appeared to be listening for what I was going to say next, so I continued. "I got the impression she doesn't want to lose me too."

I hesitated for a moment before going on. Maybe I shouldn't have brought up my mother if Candace was having a hard day. But she was just looking at me solemnly. She put down her little silver fork even though there were some clams left on her plate. She looked like she was actually listening, not just waiting for an opportunity to jump back into the conversation.

"So, I promised my Mama I'd try to be healthier. Her last friend who died ate bacon every morning like me. Of course, she was a lot older," I added. "But there's no time like the present to change your behavior. I could wait but then it might be too late. So, I just started eating turkey bacon instead. I had my first piece of turkey bacon last week and I feel better already. Maybe my body is happy that I am no longer absorbing the suffering of the pig."

Candace nodded.

That's a start," she said gently. "Though turkeys aren't treated very well either. And you still have to be careful about your health. Turkey bacon does have fewer calories, but it's still high in saturated fat which makes our cholesterol levels higher. Why don't you try some of the plant-based bacon substitutes?

They're very popular now. Sometimes the local grocery store carries them alongside the vegetables."

Just then the waitress came. Pen in hand, she asked me if I had made up my mind.

I told her I was debating between the rainbow-trout baked in parchment or the scallops.

"I would go with the scallops," said Candace. "I think the rainbow trout is served with its head on. It might stare up at us and make us feel guilty."

I didn't think there was any chance the trout would have a chance to make us feel guilty, with Candace around.

But I took my friend's advice and ordered the scallops. I didn't want to make her uncomfortable.

There was so much to catch up on with Candace. We hadn't seen each other in ages. I wanted to tell her how I had named several cows and that Cinnamon seemed to be following me around and spying on me. But first there was something that I had to ask her.

"I couldn't help noticing that you're eating clams," I observed. "Aren't clams animals too? Don't they suffer when they are sacrificed for us?"

"Sure, clams are animals and yes, they suffer. Do you have to remind me of that when I'm eating?"

Candace didn't stop to wait for an answer, so I didn't say anything. "Seafood isn't technically vegan," she continued. "It's an animal product so strict vegans don't eat it. Neither do vegetarians who eat a little wider on the spectrum. Sometimes, vegetarians eat eggs and other dairy products which are produced from animals and are not vegan.

"I like to think of myself as vegan and don't wear leather or furs or use cosmetics tested on animals. But I make an exception for seafood that doesn't have a face – especially when it is served in a restaurant like this. Isn't this place beautiful? Look at the gorgeous room around us: the high ceiling, the blue and white wallpaper with the thin stripes of gold in it, the beautiful paintings. I always feel so good about myself when I eat here."

Despite it being an upscale establishment, I was relieved I had left my leather purse at home. The day my cow had given me a look which I interpreted as a look of betrayal, I transferred all my belongings to my old vinyl purse. I hadn't used the leather purse since.

I looked at the paintings on the wall more closely. It was true that they had matching gold filigree frames which were very elegant. But the contents didn't seem like anything special. One had a tall cypress tree that rose from a swamp. Another depicted a sailboat on a placid sea. I thought both bodies of water probably were home to creatures that all had faces but that some of these faces weren't visible to us.

The room *was* comforting. It was the kind of place that suggested by its appearance that you leave your troubles at the door. It was that self-contained. The waiters and waitresses were precise and beautiful. They were slim as if food did not affect them (if they ate). They looked forever fresh-faced, young, and perfect. Come to think of it, they very much resembled the room, the crisp and pleasant wallpaper, and the paintings we were surrounded by. They were decorative containers of little substance.

When I looked around, I had seen a restaurant that I couldn't afford to eat in. But now I observed the room around me through Candace's eyes. My friend saw a place that made her feel good about herself. Why did she need this? Was the fact that she could afford to eat here reassuring? I looked at my friend solemnly and wondered at her statement. What was she telling me when she said that this place made her feel good about herself?

The waiter brought Candace's seafood linguini.

I refrained from pointing out that shrimps have faces and that her portion on the center of her gold-rimmed plate seemed small. My portion of scallops also looked scant. There were only three of them – which weren't many even if they were large. But this was a fancy restaurant, and I was my friend's guest, so I didn't point out the small portions. I didn't want to be seen as being critical.

When Candace remarked that it was a shame that Ainsley couldn't make it, I simply agreed. I wasn't forthcoming but judging from Ainsley's obviously made-up excuse, I would say that I am the more forgiving one.

I wasn't frank, so I didn't tell Candace that her behavior was often off-putting. I tended to think before I spoke, and with Candace, I thought extra hard.

We made small talk and then excitedly Candace interrupted herself and said she had something to tell me before she forgot to.

She told me about something called a farm sanctuary where the woman who ran it treated the cows like companions. She said the woman used to work on a dairy farm, got disgusted at the treatment of cows, and one day left to create a farm sanctuary. It sounded very strange. It was the first time I had heard of such a thing. I could just hear the other farmers and even people I loved, like Ainsley, dismissing it. But it also sounded like the most natural thing in the world. It sounded like where I was headed. Hope glimmered but then reality set in. I could barely pay the taxes as it was. Still...

"I would like to meet her. She sounds fascinating," I responded.

Chapter Ten

The day started like any other day. After sleeping in my narrow slot in the stinking barn, I woke up to one of the farmhands – not the one with the ham sandwich in his overalls, the nicer one who patted my side and said 'thatta girl'— ushering me to follow the herd into the field. The sun was still a pale wash of sky. The grass was long and sweet. The birds were already lined up on their wire in the sky.

I took my morning dump in the pasture. I used to go in the barn until about six months ago. Then one day I stopped. I still had to go first thing but held it in because I refused to make the barn smell worse. The stench had gotten worse in the past month or so. It now smelled so bad my sphincter slammed shut in the barn. I had to wait until I was in the pasture until I could go. This morning I went not once but twice. What a relief. I do have four stomachs and a rather large and complex intestinal system. But I am regular.

I was standing by myself, pondering the nature of dung and how my excrement would eventually become part of the earth that grew the grass I would eat, when I heard a rumbling in a different section of my stomach area. My four stomachs are proportionate to my large body. I had given up on the idea of losing weight. Who ever heard of a vain cow? Besides, the farmhands always seemed to see me when I tried to stay in the pasture (so I assume it wouldn't matter if I lost weight or not), and they made me line up with the others to be milked. One called me sneaky and the other farmhand, the one who usually carried a ham sandwich in the front pocket of his overalls, said a "fat cow" like me could never get away with being sneaky.

If I cared enough, I'd make him hear me and I'd say, "I'm not a fat cow. You're the fat cow."

Then I'd ask him how he'd like to be hooked up to the milking machine. He didn't have an udder, but I knew he had other body parts that would fit into the machine.

But that was neither here nor there, since he wasn't in the pasture where I stood that sunny morning with one of my stomachs rumbling. It rumbled and rumbled. It felt like there was something inside of me that wanted to come out.

Then I understood why it is called 'passing wind' because it felt like a tornado was let loose from inside of me. I tooted and tooted and finally, it stopped.

I was hugely relieved.

"Mooooo. That sure felt good," I said out loud. I thought I was talking to myself, since there was no one nearby to hear me. At least I didn't *think* anyone was close enough to hear me.

"Nice one. I'm *so* glad you feel better. But some of us around here are trying to breathe," said someone, sotto voce, behind me.

I could tell it was another cow from the quickness of her breath. Cows breathe faster than humans, even if we are bigger. I swung around and saw my old friend (I use the term loosely) from childhood whom I had argued with the other day in the pasture. I was going to search her out today and apologize. But with the way she was acting, I didn't think it was going to happen.

Just then I felt another rumble in my mid-section. It was in a different place than my previous rumble. The growl came from another one of my stomachs.

"Oh no," said my cow ex-friend. Even though she was standing on a summer pasture, was on thin ice with me. "It looks – no sounds and smells – like I better hurry by. But I think I can hold my breath while I stop and eat this clover."

It was true that our farts can be loud and smelly. I grazed on some sour tasting grass the previous afternoon that must have made me sick. I heard the nice farmhand telling the other one he wished the farmer could afford the more expensive sweeter grass-seed that would grow grass which would make us less gassy. He mentioned a grass called "maize silage". To my knowledge, I have never had this. It did sound tasty, and I liked the idea of the grass being sweeter. I also liked the idea of feeling better. As for the gas that comes out of me, I have never cared. I mean, it's not really my problem, except that it doesn't do anything for our image. People think cows grazing in pastures on a green hillside look so peaceful. But as the word gets out, the public will know what we're really doing as we stand there.

The farmhand said that having us eat the more expensive, sweeter grasses, would be good for the environment (that's the place we all live, not just us cows) because when we have flatulence, we emit methane gas. That's the word he used "flatulence."

I found out later from the farmer who I named Sunflower, that flatulence means the same thing as gas or farts. It's a funny word, *flatulence.*

Sunflower was talking to the farmhands and using that word. That's how I found out what it meant. She wasn't talking to me. I used to think of her as my friend. But I knew as I emitted another long fart that she wasn't really my friend. For one thing, it was obvious to me from my last expedition when I peered in her window, that she wasn't changing her ways. She was still eating the flesh of my friends. Besides, who was I kidding (not myself), Sunflower owned this farm. That meant she thought that she owned me.

My true friends were the cows I grew up with, like the one grazing on the white flowers of the clover behind me. She had been my best friend. If only she'd act more mature. I wanted to apologize to her. We were in this pasture together. We were on the same cycle for being milked and when we were done our birthing and milking cycles, we'd be in the same group of cows that were sent away together.

"Oh, God," my childhood friend uttered. Then she fell over with her four legs sticking out straight in front of her.

I thought she was making a comment about the stench of my farts.

"Better out than in," I remarked, trying to make light.

She said nothing.

I wanted to apologize but at this rate...

Wait.

Something *was* wrong. I looked in her eyes. They were open, but staring and vacant. Her feet and her wide chest were shaking.

My first impulse was to run for help, but she was moving her jaw. She seemed to be saying something to me. I leaned down so I could hear her.

"I'm sorry," she mumbled.

"You're sorry!? I'm the one who's sorry. I was going to tell you today, but then when I saw you …"

"I know, I know. I was being a jerk. Maybe it was because I wasn't feeling so hot.…"

She rolled her head back. Her eyes were extra wet.

"I'm sorry, I'm sorry. There's no one I love better than you. You're my best friend in the whole wide world." As I spoke, my eyes started to well up, too.

"I love you too," she gasped.

"Oh, stop crying," she said softly. "When you cry, it makes me want to cry and that doesn't help anything."

When I heard the word help, I snapped back to my initial impulse.

"I'll be right back," I told her.

Then I ran as fast as the wind, faster than I knew I could run.

"Whoa there, girl. What's going on?" the nice farmhand lifted the latch to the pasture and followed me back as I ran down the sloping hill.

"Oh. Something *is* wrong," he said as he bent down to attend to my friend.

Of course, something is wrong, I thought to myself.

Did he think I am out running for my health?

He moved his fingers in front of her eyes. He patted her stomach, and coaxed:

"Get up girl. We can't have people thinking you're sick because then they'll send you away. I've gotten used to seeing your silly mug around here. I'll miss you."

He coaxed and cajoled, but to no avail. My friend from childhood was not getting up.

The other farmhand, who usually had a ham sandwich in the front pocket of his overalls, ambled toward us. I welcomed his presence this time. Maybe he could help.

"I can't get her to stand," said the first farmhand as he moved to his knees next to my friend.

"Come on, girl," said the second farmhand, without conviction.

He sighed and said, "It was bound to happen. It's been a while since we had to send away a sick animal. It was just a matter of time before we'd have to do it again."

Again! This happened before?!

Then he said, in my direction – as if he were talking to me – "That's life, right? Just be glad that it wasn't you – this time. We'll be sending you away, too, eventually."

"Hey, wait a minute," said the first farmhand, still on his knees. "That isn't helping."

The standing farmhand shrugged. His bulky shoulders tugged at his denim overalls. "It could be anything – listeria, rabies. It could be fatal."

He was silent for a moment and then said, "Jody isn't going to like this."

Jody!? Who was Jody? I thought. *I had to run and find Sunflower.*

I ran up the gentle slope of the pasture.

When I saw her, I remembered Jody was their name for Sunflower.

I was in luck! I saw Sunflower walking on the other side of the fence. It looked like she was going to her silver pickup in the driveway. *No!* I thought, loudly.

I felt winded. So, I stopped and caught my breath.

Then I started mooing. I was bellowing really. Anything to get Sunflower's attention.

Follow me, I thought, loudly.

Sunflower changed direction, walked toward me, unlatched the gate, and said, "Why is that cow lying like that in the field?"

We both galloped down the hill and arrived at my friend's side in no time.

"What's going on?" Sunflower asked the farmhands.

It didn't sound good. I turned my big brown eyes up to Sunflower to see what she could do.

"I want to do what I can for her. But I'm afraid that's not much. We have to send her away before she infects the entire herd, but I can't afford a large animal veterinarian." As she talked, Sunflower began stroking my nose, the way I usually like it.

I continued to look up at her and pleaded with my eyes. My chest throbbed. My eyes were tearing up.

"I'm sorry Cinnamon. I know she's your special friend and that you've been together since you were both babies."

Despite the circumstances, my heart leapt. Sunflower knew something about me! She knew that I had a special friend. But what she didn't know was that I was determined to get what I wanted.

"I'm sorry Cinnamon. Look, if it was you, I'd borrow the money."

There was a way!

I bent my knees and knelt on all fours on the ground next to my sick friend and bellowed with all my might.

Chapter Eleven

I stood with some other cows and watched as the farmhands followed Sunflower's orders and went to get the forklift so my friend could be transported. One farmhand opened the gates so the other rode could drive his forklift through the open gates and down the hill. The man who had opened the gate, closed it, and followed the forklift as it descended in the sloping pasture. He lurched down the gently sloping hill to where the forklift was idling. The farmhand driving the forklift was the pleasant one. On foot behind him, was the farmhand who traveled with a ham sandwich in his pocket. Even though I didn't care for him, I was happy to see him. I thought that maybe he could help.

The first farmhand got out of the forklift. It took the two of them to get my cow friend onto a flat wooden box covered with canvas. They pushed and prodded, all the while groaning and wheezing. Finally, she was lying with her legs straight out in front of her on the box covered with canvas that sat on the prongs of the forklift.

"I'll have to drive extra slow so that if we hit a bump she doesn't fall off and break a leg," the nice farmhand said.

The nasty farmhand sneered with his entire face.

In case anyone didn't know his thoughts, he said, "This is a waste of my time."

That's all he said. He made a grating sound in his throat and spit.

Then on foot, with an ambling and lurching gait, he followed the forklift as it made its way slowly up the low hill.

I watched as the forklift came to a stop at the wooden gate. The farmhand on foot caught up with him and opened the wooden gate. The forklift with my friend laying on the front drove through. The driver swung his substantial arm and hand out the side as he motioned for the other farmhand (I had started thinking of him as Ham Sandwich around that time) to hold onto my cow friend as he raised the prongs to put her box into the back of the silver pickup. Then he turned back and closed the gate to the pasture.

Sunflower was standing by the back of the truck, motioning with her arms.

I could see the two men straining as they pushed my cow friend into the back of the pickup. Then they put the gate up across the back of the pickup and latched it.

My other cow friend and I were both sad as we watched the nice farmhand get into the driver's side, slam the door behind him, and wait for Ham Sandwich to slide into the passenger side. I tried to focus on keeping a positive thought for her – to see her coming back in such fine form that she would be prancing with us in the pasture again. It was hard because I was extremely sad to see her go and felt very alone in the pasture.

I remember thinking what if my friend never came back? What if she never got better? I had surmised they were taking her to get better, but I really hadn't known. The first farmhand, the one who did the driving, had been gentle enough for me to see that he cared. But the second one – if it were up to Ham Sandwich, they might dump her by the side of the road somewhere and then go out and have cow burgers for lunch. Then I remembered Sunflower had gotten into the smaller car and was driving behind them.

If my cow friend didn't come back, I didn't think I could take daily life in the pasture, the milking machine, and the farmhand's arm up my you know what so that I could get pregnant again and continue to give milk for another year. I didn't even think of the fact that even if my cow friend had come back, we would both be sent away at the same time. We would probably become lunch for some humans. I had never thought about it before, but it must have given me comfort to know I'd be sent away with my friend. Thinking about being sent away by myself, made me terrified. I couldn't face it alone.

If my cow friend didn't come back, there would be no use for me to go on. It felt like the sun would no longer rise.

I wasn't alone in being sad.

I had my other friend – the one whom I had stood next to as we watched our mutual cow friend get taken away. But each was closer friends with our friend who had left than with each other.

Because we were each so close with our cow friend who had left, we were jealous and wary of each other when she was around, even though we all pranced together. We both wanted to be her best friend. I *thought* I was her best friend, until the *other* friend came around. Watching the other friend prance with her made me wonder. *Was I the most important one?*

I imagined our other friend felt the same way. It wasn't as though we disliked each other, only that we didn't trust each other because each of us wanted to be the one that our friend loved more. It was selfish of both of us, really.

Then suddenly, after our mutual friend fell ill, all we had was each other. Nothing mattered anymore. I decided that if my sick friend stopped eating, then I would stop eating. Maybe she was refusing food right now – wherever she was. The sky was clear blue, and the weather was just starting to get cooler. Autumn appeared to be coming. But as far as I was concerned, the sky could have been gray and overcast. It could have been threatening to rain and been as humid as a fresh cow pie.

I wondered how it could be that my best friend was here one day – prancing around with her two best friends — and then gone. Come to think of it, she had been walking in circles before we had come up to her. She had been looking a little under the weather. She may have been already sick, but it looked like she had wanted to play. I wanted to play also and so did our other friend.

So, we had danced in circles, just like always. I and our other friend danced around the one we each claimed as our best friend. We danced around and around until we got tired and went back to grazing. Our other friend wandered off first and found some shade to sit in.

Aha, I had thought. I seized my opening, or what I thought was an opportunity. My cow friend was still walking in circles. I had pranced around her. *This is my chance*, I had thought, *to prove I am really her best friend.* I felt triumphant then. But after I knew she was sick, I just felt guilty. I hadn't even stopped to think that she might be sick. I had been putting myself first.

Chapter Twelve

"It looks like a case of listeriosis," said Dr. Holt, a thirty-something woman, one of two large animal veterinarians in town.

On the way in, I was greeted by a cement sculpture of a pig just outside the front door. Ainsley was working at home today, so I took our second vehicle – a navy Honda Civic – and drove behind my silver pickup. After I had made sure that Bob and Jimmy could unload my sick cow and that the man from the large animal veterinarian hospital was there to help, I returned to the front door.

I knew it would be a while until the cow was examined and diagnosed. I leaned over and studied the cement sculpture. It was unmistakably pig-like with its upturned snout, round head, squinty accusing piggy eyes, and folded-over ears. Its body was made of circles, a rounded back with parenthetical-shaped creases in it. The stone pig was crouched down on round hooves. It was so lifelike in its rendering – despite being gray instead of pink – that I got the impression if I turned it over and looked at its underbelly, the details would continue.

Once or twice, previously, I had a farmhand come in with an animal. This was the first time I had come myself with both farmhands. It was lucky that their schedules had overlapped today and that they were both working.

The reason I was here was that the cow I brought in was important to Cinnamon, and Cinnamon was important to me. I had committed the cardinal sin, Mama had long warned me about and the adults advised against in 4-H clubs. I had become attached to a farm animal.

I wondered briefly how Dr. Holt had become a large animal veterinarian. Had she grown up on a farm like me? She must love cows to do this type of work. Right?

"What's the prognosis?" I asked.

She looked at me with such utmost seriousness that I could never imagine her telling a joke. She had shoulder-length, dark curly hair brushing the shoulders of her white veterinarian's smock. She looked at me calmly and compassionately with her big brown eyes. She reminded me of one of my cows.

"I haven't examined her thoroughly yet. But I have looked her over, and I can tell already that it won't be cheap or easy," she answered. "I can give you a round of bovine antibiotics that you can give to her at the farm, but the disease may be communicable to other bovines. She might have to be quarantined for a few months. But she will most likely get better. That is if you want her too..." she paused.

I raised my eyebrows and looked at her inquisitively.

"She looks like she is in the middle of her breeding and milking cycle," said the vet. Then she took a deep breath. "So, it may not be worth it to you to cure her unless – "

Dr. Holt hesitated as if she was thinking about what she was going to say next. She looked at me as if assessing whether I could afford this. I was sure she dealt with lots of farmers who had to think about the bottom line before they agreed to any treatment. I wasn't one of the desperate farmers, but I was almost one of them. If it wasn't for the fact that Ainsley had lent me more money, I wouldn't be here.

"Unless what?"

"Look, none of us are involved with cattle because we're just interested in making money – at least not around these parts. I was raised on a farm, and I bet you were too. I care about the cows, and I've seen..." She stopped talking as if she was afraid of what I might think of her.

"What? What have you seen?" I was getting impatient, but I was also intrigued.

What was she trying to say and why was she afraid to say it?

"What I was going to say …" she shored up her shoulders in her white veterinarian's smock.

I could imagine her presenting the scientific evidence for her argument in a veterinary college.

"… is that some people grow attached to their cows. It's no longer just business for them."

I was silent. But I didn't want her to stop talking. I had to say something to encourage her to continue.

"Really?"

It wasn't a skeptical comment or even a polite one. I was curious. I really wanted to know more.

"It's controversial," she added. "But it's a reality. I've seen enough people who feel this way. It's not uncommon."

"What's not uncommon?" I asked. I was aware that I was treating the veterinarian like a skittish farm animal, maybe a yearling who was big enough to run. I was afraid she'd bolt.

"Their feelings," she added. "More than a few of my clients care for their cows so much that they have started treating them like pets."

"Pets?"

A cow was a huge pet. When I thought of a pet, I thought of Tangerine, our orange house cat. He always seemed to be in the room that I planned to enter. In other words, she seemed to know where I was going.

"Yes, pets. It's natural for humans to bond with animals. We're both mammals. Human females are equipped to produce milk and nurse our young – just like dairy cows. There is plenty of pornography portraying women being treated like farm animals. Fortunately, human women aren't actually subjected to the same treatment as cows."

I felt my jaw drop. The connections between farm animals and humans went deeper than I thought.

"So, I'm not crazy."

"No, you're not. Most of us who work with animals do so because livestock is what we know. Farming is in our blood. We've been taught ever since we can remember that cows and pigs and other animals are bred to be slaughtered, to be eaten by humans. But it's also natural to form a bond with animals, to pick up on their emotions, and to understand when they are suffering and to want to help."

"Farm animals have emotions?"

I knew this to be true, but for some reason was amazed that others knew it too.

"They sure do. It's scientifically proven. Haven't you heard the expression, 'Don't cross a cow'? They can hold grudges for years, recognize a familiar and friendly face, and plot against anyone who treats them badly. They also tend to get very attached to a few other cows, just like we may have friends that we see on a regular basis."

I thought about Candace.

Maybe some of the cows also ignored the traits in their friends they didn't care for, said a voice in my head.

I nodded and said, "The cow that I brought in is the friend of a cow who is special to me, who I just named Cinnamon."

The vet nodded seriously as if I had just described something clinical to her.

"I like that name, Cinnamon. I bet she's a special being. You know, you're not the first dairy farmer to name her cows."

Dr. Holt smiled.

I took the smile as an invitation to ask her a question.

"I'm curious – why did you become a large animal veterinarian?"

"I grew up on a farm, like I told you. When I was a girl – before I was a teen and was assigned chores. I used to take long walks by the pastures. Then one day I started singing to the cows."

"Did you sing before that?"

"Sure. I used to sing in the shower, but the cows were the first beings I ever sang to. They seemed to love my singing. They would stop grazing and look up at me. A few even mooed at me after I was done. I felt like they were asking for an encore."

"Why didn't you become a singer?" I asked.

"In junior high, I joined the chorus. We sang here and there – once at the community fair and once at the local high school. But my folks needed money to help them with the farm. And I was good at math and science. There are very few professional singers who make it. So, I took out a loan and went to veterinary school. And here I am. I love being a large animal vet. I love helping the animals get better. There's nothing I'd rather be doing – including singing on a stage. But now I see family farms going out of business. The farmers who are still around, often can't afford to give their animals the proper care."

She paused and looked at me sadly.

"I've seen people leave crying because they can't afford to give their farm animal the proper course of treatment. I used to run a tab for people who couldn't afford care for their animals. My grandfather used to do the same thing. But like him, I finally couldn't afford this anymore. I lost too much money."

Dr. Holt paused and sighed.

"I wonder what is going to happen to the farmers. Sometimes I wonder what is going to happen to me. But I keep telling myself to hang on for at least five years because my parents will be retired by then, so I won't need to help them with the farm. Also, I'll have my tuition loans paid off."

"I'm sure you'll be really good at whatever you do," I said. I smiled and looked encouragingly at her.

"Thank you," she said.

Then she shifted into a more professional mode.

"If Cinnamon's cow friend is the one who is sick," she stated without missing a beat, "you'll want to do everything you can to help her get better to keep Cinnamon happy. As you probably have witnessed, cows form strong bonds with their cow friends."

I nodded.

"She is mid-way in her birthing and milking cycle. You were correct in your observation," I told her. "But my cows are more than just milk producers to me," I continued.

"That's good," said the doctor.

"There's been a lot of research done lately on the emotions of cows," she stated. "They're wonderful creatures with their own distinct personalities. Some are shy. Others are outgoing. They're just like us and it takes an exceptional human to connect with them."

As she spoke, I looked around the office. The wallpaper, bluish gray with a white flower print, soothed me. A photograph of a brown and black brindle cow with its brown nose upturned was framed on the wall. Behind the cow's head was a cloudless deep sky blue that seemed to stretch into forever. The cow was standing in a pasture that was part of a farm. It could have been my pasture, my farm. I was filled with pride for keeping it going. Papa would have been proud. After he died, the farm was pretty much what kept me going – that and Ainsley. I still had Mama too, but it wasn't the same with Papa gone.

Next to the framed photograph of the brindled cow was an adorable watercolor of a pink pig with an upturned snout. The pig looked healthy and happy. Maybe that's the way pigs were supposed to look.

I felt a twinge of guilt. I wouldn't have sold my hog if I hadn't needed the money. I should have swallowed my pride and asked Ainsley if I could borrow the money – even if I hadn't fully paid the last loan back.

"You know cows can live up to fifteen or twenty years," commented Dr. Holt. "That's almost as long as a horse can live, and I've seen people who are very attached to their horses."

"I had no idea that a cow could live that long," I said. "To tell you the truth, I never even thought about it."

Suddenly I felt sick.

Chapter Thirteen

The same day my cow friend was taken away, she came back. It was the time of day when you know the sun will set but it hasn't yet. The sky was still light, but it was quite pale. The sun was a bright yellow line with pooled magenta hovering over it on the western horizon. I could see it through the line of trees behind the pasture. It was almost milking time. Under other circumstances, I would have been glad the farmhands were gone. I really hated being hooked up to those milking machines, not to mention having to stand in cramped quarters in the smelly barn.

Me and my other cow friend stood erect on all fours, poised to start prancing with her. Expectation was in the air. We stood higher, our backs and bellies slouching less. We were happy she was back and wanted to play.

We went up the slight incline of the pasture to stand just inside the wooden fence so that we could greet our friend. After the silver pickup came into the driveway, there was another crunch of tires on the gravel behind it as the small navy car driven by the farmer came to a halt.

Sunflower slammed the car door behind her and hurried over to the back of the pickup. She stood and watched as the farmhands unlatched the pickup's back gate and took the sick cow out of the back with the help of the forklift.

She was still laying down on her side with her feet extended.

It looked like they had put her on a piece of sturdy canvas. They tugged and tugged. I imagined the farmhands huffing and puffing.

She didn't come to greet us. In fact, she didn't come into the pasture at all.

The farmhands had put her back on the front prongs of the forklift. The driver got into the forklift, lowered the prongs, and then drove her slowly – with her legs still straight in front of her – to the fenced-in area around the vegetable stand.

"I hope she's okay," the other cow had sniffed, more to herself than to me.

I felt the same way but suffered in silence.

On top of everything, I felt guilty about the argument I had with my cow friend the other day. I especially felt bad about telling her I was special because the farmer had named me. If I had to pick sides (and this was one of those times), I would always be on the side of the bovines and not the humans. I didn't care if the farmer could read my thoughts when I put my mind to it, I was still better friends with my childhood cow friend.

I backed away from the fence, away from the farmer. I noticed that my other cow friend followed me. We walked some ways and turned around to see what the farmer was doing.

Sunflower, apparently, had taken our backing away to heart. Or maybe she was deeply and genuinely concerned about our cow friend. She had gone inside the fenced-in area and was kneeling, then sitting, on the ground in front of our cow friend.

Without realizing it, I had moved closer to our mutual cow friend. I was standing so close to her that we could swat the flies from each other's flanks. I almost bent my head down to graze. But then I kept my head up. Grazing was just a habit. I wasn't hungry. Usually, I could always eat.

This was more than a determination not to eat. I had really lost my appetite.

Chapter Fourteen

The following Sunday I was in church singing hymns and thinking about cows. There was another guest minister. It was summer and the regular minister was on an extended vacation. I looked up at the stained-glass windows and wondered who made them. I had heard some of the windows were brought here on a flatbed truck. One of the scenes depicted the baby Jesus in a manger with golden straw sticking out of his cradle and an equally golden halo circling his tiny head. This prompted me to wonder:

What does it mean that the baby Jesus is always depicted as being born in a barn?

I closed my eyes and pictured the rest. In those days, a stable would have housed many different animals. The cows would be mooing, and nearby a pen of full-grown sheep would be staring. It was winter, so their coats would look like puffy clouds around narrow heads. Sheep usually gave birth in the Spring so some of the sheep mamas would be expecting. The uncomfortable ones would be baa-ing.

I thought about their lambs becoming Easter dinner and shuddered. Personally, I had never cared for lamb. I probably never ate lamb because ever since I can remember, I watched them bleating and following their mamas around. But I had sat at the same tables as people eating lamb and never said anything. I hadn't wanted to be impolite. But now I wondered.

This guest minister was talking about the oneness of everything. So far, she hadn't mentioned animals. They must be part of the oneness, right?

If people ate animals, didn't they think the animals were below them or less than them? Wasn't it arrogant that people thought animals were here to be eaten by them?

I shook my head to come out of my daydream and forced myself to pay attention.

The minister mentioned Jesus lived inside of us and was not separate from us. I agreed but wondered if Jesus was a vegetarian. Was Jesus vegan?

I think I had heard somewhere that Jesus was a vegetarian. But I remembered the story where he caught and ate fish.

I had learned that vegetarians who ate fish were called "pescatarians."

Maybe Jesus just ate fish and other seafood on special occasions like Candace.

I wondered what kind of food they served at the last supper.

Most of the traditional Passover food was vegetarian. In fact, except for the lamb shank bone and the egg, the traditional foods were entirely vegan. If it wasn't for the egg that I ate that morning in my French toast, I could feel self-righteous about not eating any animal products. I was in church, after all. What better place to feel self-righteous? I did feel full of myself to the point of overflowing, but then I came down with a thud. Who was I to feel the lightning bolt of self-righteousness shoot through me? I was only a common dairy farmer. I knew what happened to my animals even if I didn't want to talk about it.

What about the Biblical commandment: "Thou shalt not kill"?

I pictured a ceremonial Passover plate with six circles in it, labeled for the traditional bitter herbs, greens, horseradish, egg, and lamb-shank bone. The lamb-shank bone would have been a problem for Jesus if he didn't eat meat. Maybe instead of a lamb shank, that part of his (I normally would capitalize the "h" but if we were all one, there was no need for capitalization) plate contained rice and beans. At the restaurant when Candace was eating seafood, she had told me about combining plant foods to make proteins. I forgot most of what she said. But I remember her saying that rice and beans make a complete protein. I also remember her saying that protein was overrated and that it wasn't so hard to get protein from a plant-based diet and that most vegetables provided protein all by themselves.

The minister finished her sermon and started to lead us in prayer.

"Dear Mother-God and Father-God," she said.

The guest minister, a colleague of the regular minister, was a young woman from another church and I hadn't heard her preach before.

I had never heard anyone say "Mother-God and Father-God" before. It sounded strange and made me vaguely uncomfortable. I took a deep breath and felt the cool air-conditioned air of the sanctuary fill me. I shifted in the pew, looked up, and smiled at the man sitting next to me. I hadn't seen him before. Despite the heat outside, he wore a suit and tie. His hair was cropped, and his dark brown skin made the glint from the earpiece of his metallic gold glasses more visible. He smiled back. I decided I liked "Mother-God and Father-God" despite it sounding odd. Maybe this was something only the guest minister said.

I never thought of God as anything but God. But I guess I was thinking of "God, the Father." That's what I had been taught. Thinking of God as the father made me think of my own father. He may have had his faults (like his smoking) but he was a good man.

But God didn't necessarily have to be a father. Maybe the minister was right, maybe there was a Mother God also. *Religion wasn't so bad,* I thought, *even if many of the things people said about it – the reasons why they avoided it – were true.* I thought about Ainsley. I hadn't even bothered to ask Ainsley to come to church with me that morning. I knew the answer. Some people had been hurt too bad by religion to ever return.

The fact was that I didn't think of God as male or female. I didn't think that men were better than women or, for that matter, that women were better than men. God was just a nice little three letter word that to me signified all that was good and necessary in life. The sun rose every day and it set. That was God. The crickets sang their song every summer to let us know that the seasons would soon be changing. God was the cricket and God was the song. I realized that I had always known that we are all one.

The minister was right to say "Mother-God and "Father-God." But what if God was genderless. What if male and female didn't matter?

Dear heavenly whatever, I thought, replacing her salutation.

But 'whatever' didn't sound right. It made the person sound like a thing – an "it." I replaced it with 'whomever.'

CINNAMON: A dairy cow's (and her farmer's) path to freedom

Dear heavenly whomever, I thought.

Then I realized that I had to think about something to pray for.

Mama was in good health, thank God. We were scraping by at the farm, thank God. But Cinnamon's friend had just come home from Dr. Holt's where she had to stay for several days while she was being treated for listeriosis. I had the hired hands put up a small area of fence that opened to the fruit stand. Then I had them fence in the stand. The fruit stand had a corrugated roof where she could stand in the shade and sleep at night in the hay that I had brought in for her. When one of the farmhands grumbled about "…the cow contaminating the vegetables and maybe even the customers," I barked at him that, "Your job is to do what I say and that's why I hired you."

It was an unusual moment of anger and authority for me. I really must have been stressed out.

I didn't bother to tell him my plan to stop selling veggies at the stand until the cow got better and could return to the pasture and the barn. It wasn't really his business, and I didn't like his attitude. It had been very hot. Irritation was more contagious than listeriosis.

We might be all one, but it was the cow I was thinking about and not the hired man.

I realized with a little shudder that I hadn't even named her.

Here I was in the house of the Lord. I could think of no better place to think of her name.

Dear God, I began, reverting to the salutation that I always used.

May Cinnamon's friend ... (and then it came to me) ... *Spice. That's her name, Spice! Thank you for her beautiful name. Cinnamon and Spice and everything nice...*

I thought of the line from the nursery rhyme or maybe it was Sugar and Spice. Either way, that's what little girls are made of – my girls.

Were they were meant to make hamburgers and veal, steaks, and disease? And in the meantime, to produce milk? Is that what they were made for? Was that their divine purpose?

I closed my eyes and squeezed them shut.

No, said a voice in my head. *They are not here for you. But you can learn something from them.*

What? I wondered.

The voice in my head was silent. I knew I would have to pay attention to the cows and learn from them.

I've heard it said that when you pray you should pray that it should be for someone or something outside of you – like world peace. This seemed impossible, and I felt like a beauty contestant for wishing it. There was so much news nowadays. I couldn't take most in.

Plus, it seemed like people were inventing their destinies. *Didn't they know that action or inaction had consequences?* It was too much for me to think about. It all seemed out of my control. All I could be certain of was having direction over was my own backyard. I ran a dairy farm and kept the rolling pastures, my twenty acres – large, but also a small amount of land for a dairy farmer – from becoming a shopping mall and a parking lot. I did not use pesticides on my vegetables, even though neighbors told me that was the only way to keep the pests away. Those vegetables were food for Ainsley and me – and neither of us wanted to eat chemicals. We wanted to taste the goodness of the land. I knew the value of land and that no more of it was being made. It may be true the costs associated with the land were hard to keep up with but, in many ways, I was the richest person I knew.

I decided to go back to praying.

May I keep your land pure. May butterflies and bees continue to thrive on it. May your creatures, the cows, and the sheep and ... well, all of them ... continue to roam in your hilly green pastures. In particular, please help Spice get better again so that she is no longer a risk to the other cows and so that she can play with her friend Cinnamon again.

Cinnamon is one of your creatures too. She is the cow friend of Spice.

Please, please, please let Spice get better.

Amen

Then it hit me like a lightning bolt. If Spice made it and was reunited with Cinnamon that would be wonderful. But I would be nurturing her only for the two more years she had left in her birth milking cycles and then she would be sent away to become…

Why was I doing this? It would have been easier to turn away and have had the vet put her to sleep. But no, I had become attached to Cinnamon. I could see that she was very upset about her friend. Cinnamon was just a cow, right? But now she had a name and her friend, Spice, had a name too.

I was wasting Ainsley's money to nurture an animal who would eventually be put to death. And God only knew when I could repay that debt.

At that moment, I sensed that things were going to have to change.

Chapter Fifteen

The days went slowly. We woke up in the smelly barn like always. Almost before we could stand, we had to endure the first milking of the day. The machines were hooked up to us, cold against our warm skin. We heard the familiar rhythm of the chugging sound. Then we were herded into the pasture.

This is how all our days started, but today was different. I was so worried about my cow friend who was ill that the milking machines didn't even bother me. In the pasture, my sick friend was all I could think about. *Would she be okay?*

My other friend from calfhood and I stood at the wooden fence facing the new wire fence that led to the farm stand. That's where our friend was. So far, she was just lying on the ground not eating or drinking when food was brought to her. The farmhand who had taken to insulting me – calling me a "fat cow" on more than one occasion – dumped the food in front of her with a loud clanging sound as the large metal bowl hit the gravel. Then he walked away.

Sunflower was out today. She saw me standing at the wooden fence and came over to greet me.

"Cinnamon," she said, scratching my nose the way I like it. "Things don't look good. I know you can't understand me, but there's only so much I can do."

I gave her the silent treatment. I wasn't going to let her know I could understand her. If I so much as moved my head, she might interpret it as a nod, a consent she had done everything she could and that I understood it was time to say goodbye.

But I wasn't giving her my consent to let my friend go. There had to be something that she could do.

My eyes welled up.

Sunflower looked down at me sadly.

"I borrowed the money and took her to the large animal vet."

I looked down and thought, *I knew that*. What did she think that I was stupid and unobservant?

Even if I didn't know what 'money' meant, I wasn't going to admit it – especially to her. 'Money' was a new word to me. It sounded like it had something to do with me. But did it?

Chapter Sixteen

The next day I felt lightheaded as I joined the other cows in the barn and marched in formation to the pasture. I had slept in the barn and stood up to endure the morning milking without eating a single strand of hay. I followed the tail end of a cow before me. I hadn't eaten a thing since my friend from childhood had come home and was quarantined and still sick. Our path passed the now fenced in area where my friend was – the area behind the vegetable stand. I couldn't see her because I was flanked by two cows slightly taller than me.

I could feel the warmth of their large bodies as I stood between them.

I craned my neck, but I still couldn't see. I couldn't bring myself to ask the cow to the right of me if she could see.

"Looks like there is no change," the cow said. It appeared she could read my mind.

I started. This cow wasn't a friend. We had eyed each other hostilely over a patch of particularly sweet-smelling long grass not too long ago. But she seemed to know that the cow in quarantine was my friend. Maybe my friend was behind me that day of the standoff over that patch of sweet-smelling grass. Perhaps she had been running down the hill to join me in eating from a new patch of grass I had found.

"She is still lying on the ground on her side with her legs out straight in front of her. It doesn't look like she has eaten," she added.

I hung my head. A tear fell from my eye.

"Don't worry," said the same cow, in a reassuring tone. "It's only a day after she came back. Maybe she'll eat something today. There's still a chance she might get stronger."

"Then again maybe she won't," said a voice to my left. "What? You don't have to look at me like that."

The first cow, on my right, who had spoken to me must be giving the cow on my left a look.

"I've seen it before," said the cow to my left. Her voice was lower. "A cow lies down and never gets up. Then they take her away. The last time I saw it happen, it occurred to me that the diseased cow was lucky. At least she gets to die in peace. Eventually all of us get taken away to the slaughterhouse. It doesn't matter if we stay healthy."

"Still, there's no reason to make someone feel worse than she already feels," said the cow on my right. "She *might* get better. I've seen it before."

"Yeah. Yeah. You've seen it all before. I know, I know," snorted the cow on my left.

"I am older and wiser than you," the voice on my right retorted.

I still had my head down. We were at a standstill. I heard a creak as the gate opened. I told myself it would be over soon. I hated being in the middle of someone else's conflict.

"I get it," snarled the voice on my left. "You're older and wiser and always have to have the last word."

"That's right," said the cow on my right.

Just in time, we started moving again. We went down the top slope of the pasture. I broke free from the other cows – no more back ends and tails in my face, no more hostile voices from cows on either side of me. I walked to a new spot where some high grass grew but I still wasn't hungry. I was so lightheaded, though, that I thought I might fall over. I looked toward my friend who was quarantined but I couldn't see her. Slowly, I lowered myself and knelt until I was perched on my four bent legs.

I closed my eyes. Crickets hummed. They sounded like autumn which was right around the corner. I used to love the changing of the seasons. It meant different smells and colors would be here soon. But when my friend became ill, it no longer mattered to me what season it was. Despite being in the doldrums, I couldn't help noticing my surroundings. The air smelled like morning – like fresh grass and the first chirping of birds. It felt like the day was new. And it was. This was the kind of morning I used to relish. Morning used to be the favorite part of my day. But now it didn't matter. Nothing mattered anymore.

I sat down because I was lightheaded and tired from not eating. But later I realized that I had sat down because my friend was lying down. I was in solidarity with her. If she was sick and wasting away, then I would continue my hunger fast also. She was my good friend and therefore a part of me. She alone knew my heart, what I was thinking, what I had been like when I was a calf, what I was going to do next. She knew my mood. She knew when I wanted to play. She would come and prance with me. She knew when the sadness came over me – when I was feeling blue because I had never met my mother or because I knew I would be sent away. In the past, my cow-friend had always known and had come and stood with me, and we breathed in and out together. She never tried to make me feel something other than what I was feeling.

She knew how it felt not to know your mother. She knew how it felt to be afraid of being sent away in the future. Like any true friend, she made me feel like more of myself. She made me feel good about myself, not bad. She was truly a friend, and a true friend was hard to find.

I was still sitting in the pasture with my eyes closed.

"Cinnamon?"

I heard a gentle whisper of a voice in front of me.

"Cinnamon are you okay? Please be okay."

My eyes flew open.

It was Sunflower. She was squatting in front of me. She had a red bandanna tied around her golden hair. She wore a button-down rumpled shirt that was the same exact bluish-purple color as a tasty periwinkle flower. Her blue jeans came to the tops of her plain navy sneakers that sunk a little into the mud of the pasture.

I was touched she had come down into the pasture. That was rare. I was also rather amazed she could identify me from the rest of the herd. But I was cautious not to be too affectionate. She was a human and, on top of that, the farmer. I still felt guilty about the argument I had with my now sick friend even though I had had a change of heart. My cow friend had been right. The farmer was our captor. I couldn't deny that anymore. The farmer was the reason we were sent away after we were done producing milk.

Despite my swirling thoughts and my lightheadedness, I managed to lift my head a little and cock my ears in Sunflower's direction.

"That's my girl," Sunflower whispered. "You still look alert. But I noticed that you're not eating and that's not good. That's why I brought you some treats – the same thing that I'm going to feed to your special friend. Look, I picked the treats especially for you from the garden."

I looked up into her face for a moment. Her face looked bigger than it usually was. Her eyes were swollen, making her brown eyes look even narrower, like seeds. There was something uncertain about her expression – as if she was seeking my approval.

"Please," she whispered.

She opened a burlap bag in front of me. Even before I looked in, I smelled apples, carrots, potatoes, turnips. I sniffed the air and caught a whiff of clover. After my hunger strike, my taste buds finally woke up. Even the cabbage and the cauliflower leaves smelled good.

I wanted to eat, but what was the point? If my friend died, then I might as well die too. I would have no one to prance with, no one to look for in the pasture. I lowered my head.

"Cinnamon, I have a plan. You have to listen, and you have to understand me," insisted the farmer.

Of course, I understood her. I always understood her. Suddenly, I was irritated. If Sunflower didn't understand that, she wasn't really my friend. She was my captor, but I liked her. With that realization, something shifted in my heart. Maybe she was somewhere between my captor and my friend. I sensed my fate had something to do with this thing called 'money.' Maybe I could help her with that.

Plus, I wanted to help my cow friend. In fact, I would do anything to help her. I was all ears.

"I want you to eat," pleaded Sunflower. I noticed she was speaking rather fervently. "And while you eat, I want you to chew very slowly and imagine your friend eating also. Her name is 'Spice' by the way. I named her Spice."

My head was still lowered, but I raised it.

Hmmm, I thought. *Cinnamon and Spice. That has a nice ring to it.*

I looked up at her earnest brown eyes.

"I have a bag here for you and an identical one for your friend Spice."

She spilled the contents of the bag before me. There were slices of fresh apples. The raw potato pieces and the turnips were cubed. Even the carrots were chopped in quarters and then in halves to make it easier for us to eat. Someone had put some effort into this. Either Sunflower had or her human friend who cooked for her. From the looks of it, both had prepared this.

I put my nose toward the contents of the bag and inhaled. I smelled apples and crispness. The treats smelled so fresh that I inhaled the goodness of the earth. My nostrils quivered with anticipation. Before I knew it, an apple slice slipped into my mouth. I swallowed sweetness. I was chewing cubes of raw potatoes and turnup. I chewed carefully feeling the food liquify, tasting the savory and sweet before I swallowed. One of my stomachs rumbled. I wondered what was coming next.

"That's a good girl. When you chew, think of your friend Spice and see her healthy and playing with you again in the pasture."

I closed my eyes and thought, *playing together? It is my favorite thing to do.*

I marveled at the fact Sunflower had even noticed. She seemed to know an awful lot about me.

I opened my eyes and watched the back of Sunflower as she walked up the hill. I hadn't seen her run in more than a year. She had grown too heavy. She was breathing hard, and I could tell that each step was an effort. But there was purpose in each step. I could tell she was going somewhere. There was an air about her that she was expecting something. I looked up to the wooden fence that enclosed the pasture and I saw her human friend standing there. The person had short brown hair and was dressed in jeans and a black shirt. I still couldn't tell if Sunflower's friend was male or female.

I ate the rest of my treats. I chewed slowly while imagining my friend Spice (that was a good name for her) eating the treats also. I saw her getting stronger and coming back to the pasture and prancing with me.

I even ate the cabbage and cauliflower leaves, although these were the least tasty of the treats. Then when I was done eating, I farted. Excuse me, I meant to say that I passed gas from one of my stomachs.

Crickets hummed around me. I was drowsy. I closed my eyes and pictured Spice sitting up on all fours like me and eating her treats. Then I saw her feeling stronger and deciding to stand on her four legs to explore the area where she was quarantined. Then I saw her become so healthy that she was glowing.

I imagined an aura of golden light all around her.

I closed my eyes and fell asleep.

I dreamed that Spice was so healthy and glowing that Sunflower noticed. Time fast forwarded in my dream and soon it was time for Spice to come out of quarantine and join us in the pasture. I dreamed that I saw her running down the hill – with the glowing light still around her. When she neared me, I was so happy that I began to prance.

The dream was so real that tufts of grass tickled my legs as I pranced in a circle. She joined me and we danced together. Around and around, we went until up was down and down was up. Was the grass the sky or was the sky the sky?

Still in my dream, we tired and stood side by side, content to eat the grass we had danced on and to swat flies with our long tails.

Everything was still. Gradually, I became aware of the crickets humming around me. Slowly, I opened my eyes.

I was still alone in my spot in the pasture. Spice was nowhere to be seen.

For a moment, I wasn't sure if I had imagined seeing her or if I fallen asleep and dreamed of her. Despite what one of cows had said that morning, I still held out hope that she would get better.

One of my stomachs grumbled. I was hungry. Now that my hunger strike was broken, I thought about finding some tall grass to graze on. But first, there was something I wanted to do.

I rose on my four legs. My knees were kind of creaky after sitting on the cool ground so long, but as I strode up the sloping hill of the pasture, I felt so good that I broke into a run.

At the top of the hill, I paused since the wooden fence was in front of me. I was near the opening where we were herded into the pasture each morning.

I peered over to where Spice was. At first, I couldn't see because the thin planks of the wooden fence were in my way. So, I ducked my head under the top and stuck my face through. I stared and stared in the direction of the wire fence that enclosed Spice – the fenced in area that included the now deserted vegetable stand.

I blinked. At first, I thought that what I saw was just what I wanted to see.

It was a miracle.

Spice was sitting up on all fours. Every now and then she lowered her head to her metal bowl.

It looked like she was eating!

She had taken the first step to getting better.

I was so happy that I mooed loudly – saying, "Good girl!"

I imagined that I bellowed loud enough for everyone to hear me: the birds sitting on the wire that framed the sky, the sheep in their pens and the other cows dotting the pasture.

I had bellowed this loud before – in sadness. But this bellow was full of the higher and the extraordinarily happy tones of joy.

The sky became bluer. The green grass shimmered. The world rejoiced with me.

I looked down and saw a spider asleep in the middle of its web. The morning dew was still sparkling on the strands.

The spider looked like it was sleeping.

It suddenly occurred to me that the spider may have been keeping watch over my friend when I couldn't. She may even have been transmitting my dreams and my hopes to Spice while I was sleeping.

She was probably weaving her web then. Maybe it was her web that held the world together.

I didn't want to disturb her while she was sleeping, so I whispered and in a soft voice said, "Thank you."

Chapter Seventeen

"I'm glad you changed your diet, but you're still heavy. You don't look like yourself. I can't help but wonder..."

"What, Mama?"

It was Thursday. I was once again visiting Mama at the retirement home on the outskirts of town. We were going to have lunch, but I told Mama I was no longer eating dairy, red meat, or pork and was trying to avoid chicken and turkey. Mama said I had too many dietary restrictions to eat at the home. (I figured that it was too complicated to explain the word "vegan" to her.) So, we visited after lunch. It was a nice day – in the middle seventies – right before autumn and we sat outside on our usual bench.

I wasn't hungry because I ate a protein bar in the pickup on the way. I had told myself that the protein bar was the only thing I was going to eat that morning and afternoon, but then I stopped at the convenience store and bought a full-size bag of chips. Ruffles. *Mmmm. My favorite.* I told myself that I was only going to eat a quarter of the bag. The chips were so salty and crispy that they were gone before I knew it. After I ate a quarter of the bag, I told myself that I was only going to eat half the bag. Before you know it, the empty bag lay on the seat next to me, rumpled and shiny.

"What, Mama? You know you can ask me anything," I replied.

"I just wonder…"

I nodded.

"I wonder if you're happy," she asked.

"Of course, I'm happy Mama," I replied automatically.

I had been ecstatic Spice had gotten better, served out her quarantine time, and that she was grazing again with the herd. But at the same time, something was nagging at me. At first, I couldn't identify it. I mostly stayed in the house. But Ainsley tried to shoo me out – telling me I was in a funk. Finally, when I went down to the pasture to check on Spice and had petted her long nose just the way I had done when she was getting better, it came to me. I had nursed her back to health so she and Cinnamon could be reunited. But in just a few years, they would end up as someone's lunch. Then I remembered I first had this thought at church. I must have tried to forget it after the service when someone asked me how I was, and I replied, "fine."

Since then, I had trying to pretend that everything was

fine – that I could keep on doing things the way they always had been done. Apparently, I thought that my feelings in church would stay there. So, everything was fine and then I was in a funk. Knowing why I felt the way I did, didn't make me feel any better.

"It doesn't seem like you're happy," commented Mama.

"Why shouldn't I be happy?" I replied. "I'm doing what I've always wanted to do."

"What's that?" asked Mama.

"You know. I love animals – especially cows. Papa loved them too. I'm keeping the farm going in memory of Papa."

"But what your Papa wanted most was for you to be happy," replied Mama.

"I am happy," I persisted.

"One of the happiest moments of my life…" – I stopped and looked at Mama. "I mean, of my adult life, was when I released Spice from quarantine and led her back to the pasture."

"Spice?" Mama looked confused.

"Spice is the name that I gave the cow who is the best friend of Cinnamon," I replied.

"Cinnamon?"

"That's what I named my cow friend. Cinnamon was really upset when Spice got sick." I replied.

"Oh, so you're naming the cows. No wonder you're getting attached to them," Mama replied dryly.

"First, I named Cinnamon, and then I named her friend, Spice, when she got sick. She was really sick. I was afraid she was going to die. I was just going to let nature take its course, but then I saw how sad Cinnamon was. So, I borrowed the money from Ainsley and went to the large animal veterinarian in town."

"How is Ainsley?" asked Mama cautiously.

"Fine," I replied.

There was an awkward silence between us. I didn't tell her that Ainsley was worried about being in the next round of layoffs at the firm. Ainsley had a flexible schedule and wasn't about to find that again. I noticed the worry about being laid off was replacing the complaining about the paperwork and the pettiness of the small-minded co-workers.

Mama knew I relied on Ainsley for loans to keep the farm going. She knew I was grateful, but she still didn't budge. My relationship with Ainsley had long been a sore spot with Mama. She didn't approve of us not being married. Once, she had told me that she thought I could do better.

"I've been thinking that I was wrong about Ainsley. Anyone who makes you happy is a good thing. Maybe since I only had one child, I thought too much about your future. Then when it was different than I imagined, I got upset over nothing. The important thing is that you have someone who loves you and cares for you."

"I do," I replied. I was surprised Mama changed her mind about Ainsley, but this was proof that everyone is capable of change.

Mama sighed and said, "You don't look happy. I didn't want to mention it, but you look bloated."

"I always get bloated before my time of the month," I said. But I felt guilty. I'm sure the salty chips didn't help any. Maybe I'd discuss my water retention problem with my doctor.

"This looks like something more," maintained Mama.

She didn't look so good herself. Usually vibrant, Mama suddenly looked like an old lady. I noticed her shuffling when she walked. Now, the bench looked bigger around her shrunken frame. There seemed to be more deep lines across her forehead. She was thirty-five years older than me, but I hadn't really thought about her getting old before. She was in her seventies now. I was worried about her after Papa died, but I didn't think about her getting older. I just worried that she would have a hard time without Papa. Mama was always just Mama. I thought of her as ageless because she was my mother. I shuddered when I thought of what had happened to my father. But my Mama had never smoked. Even though her face suddenly seemed sunken – as if her features had collapsed in on themselves – I thought she would live forever.

Mama had the stubborn look on her face that I had always hated. Her lips were set in a straight line. Her eyes narrowed. She looked like a dog with a bone. Her features seemed to emit a low growl.

I knew she couldn't be fooled. I decided to come clean.

"There has been something bugging me," I admitted. "But it's not Ainsley who is making me unhappy."

I told her about Spice getting sick and me nursing her back to health, only to have thoughts about her being sent away in another few years. I told her I felt split. I loved animals – so I wanted to be near them and being a farmer was the way to be with cows. But I hated the thought of what became of them. Suddenly, it had become intolerable to me.

"I told your father we should have sold the farm and given you the money," said Mama.

"This is why I didn't want to tell you. You always blame yourself. Believe me, Mama, this is not your fault."

"I know. I know," sighed Mama. "We tried to do the best thing for you. But we should have known. I remember when you were a child, and you were upset when you found out what happened to the cows after they stopped giving milk. You were young then, about ten. We wanted to wait until we told you."

I nodded and replied, "I remember that. I thought the cows were my friends and that they would live forever. I thought you and Papa would live forever, too."

Despite my best efforts, my eyes moistened. A tear tickled my cheek.

A wave of sadness crossed Mama's face.

"We were so heartbroken you were sad. We agreed you were right. It's hard to see our animal friends get slaughtered… but…" Mama's voice trailed off.

"We were just doing what we were taught," she continued. "Both of us were raised on farms. We loved the land, and we loved the animals. So, when grandma left your aunt and me the land, I bought my sister out. My sister never did care a lick for farming. She ran off just as soon as she could – with the first man who came along. I loved farming and so did your Papa. We kept the farm going even though he had to take a job to make ends meet."

"You did the right thing, Mama. I couldn't imagine life without the animals and the land. I would have never known

Cinnamon and Spice without the farm. The last time I remember being happy was when I decided Spice was well enough to leave quarantine and go down and join the others in the pasture. She went straight to Cinnamon. I could tell they were both happy since they were reunited and would be with each other. But then it hit me. I had only nursed Spice back to health so that she could keep giving milk. Then in two years or so, both Cinnamon and Spice would be sent away. So now…"

"Now, it isn't working," Mama replied gently.

I shook my head sadly.

"It really isn't. I used to love being outside every day. I used to look forward to feeding the animals and I especially enjoyed milking the cows. Even after the machines came, I loved walking past the pasture and seeing the cows every day. But now it feels like everywhere I look, I see misery. I used to pet the sheep and was always amazed at how fluffy their coats were. Now when I go to the sheep barn, they seem to stare at me accusingly. I know that many of them are pregnant and that most of their lambs will become Easter din … well, you know.

"And the cows," I continued. "They look at me judgmentally, too. Just this morning, I poked my head in the barn and a big brown and white Guernsey glared at me. I felt guilty that I could leave the barn of my own accord, and she couldn't. She had a chain over her head to make her stay in her milking area. I talked to one of the farmhands and he told me that the more difficult cows have to be chained so they don't bolt while they are giving milk. I know it sounds crazy, but I feel like I can sense the cows' emotions. First, they were just cows. Then I gave one a name. And now I'm a mess."

I broke down sobbing. I had told Mama far more than I meant to. I had said things I hadn't known I felt.

"You're not a mess and you're not crazy," said Mama in a voice deeper than her usual speaking voice. It sounded like it came from a long hollow inside of her.

"Life is short," she continued. "In many ways, it's just like the song that I used to sing when I took your arms in mine and sang, 'Merrily, merrily, merrily, life is like a dream.' Life *is* like a dream when you're doing what you love. It's not worth it, if you're just going through the motions. Believe me, I know. Your father and I were just going through the motions in the several years before he retired. We were tired of farming but wanted to save the farm. It was like a special person to us. The farm had been in our family for generations. The land was a lineage. We couldn't lose it. It would be like losing our family history. We loved the land. We felt like we belonged to the land, like we had sprung from it – like Adam and Eve in the Bible when they were made from dust. I know this must seem crazy to you."

I just shook my head. What she said made sense to me.

"That's when I got rid of the chickens. It just wasn't worth it for the few eggs that they laid. I put an ad in the local shopper and found a poultry farmer who wanted to buy them.

"What I mean to say, is that you should always pursue your passions. Life is full of people who may think they don't have passions or that they are unable to pursue them. When people don't pursue their passions, something happens to them. I've seen it. They do what they think they are supposed to do. Then when they aren't happy, they become rigid. The time to change is right now, before it's too late."

I wiped my eyes.

"But Mama what was your passion? You told me that you loved the farm – the animals and the land – but ...?"

Apparently, Mama didn't want to hear the rest of the question.

"There was your father and then there was you. We tried for five years before we got pregnant. We were planning on adoption but then you came along. I know that society expects women to give birth. But I really *wanted* to have you. It's something I did for myself – as much as for you. But we *never* wanted you to feel trapped. The farm was *our* life. Now, you're free to create *your* life."

We were silent for a moment. I remembered Papa telling me that Mama played the piccolo and wanted to go to Julliard

School in New York. But she was turned down for a scholarship and her parents couldn't afford to send her, so she stayed home, married Papa, and sold the piccolo. Mama and Papa had met at a local dance when they were teens but didn't start courting seriously until they were both finished high school. Then they got engaged and married. I came along some years later when they were in their mid-thirties. That meant I was practically a late-in-life baby – at least around these parts. That's how I got here. So much in life depends on fate.

I was quiet for another moment.

"The farm was *my* life too," I reminded her, finally breaking the silence. "I grew up there with you and because I grew up on our family farm, I will always have a special feeling for the animals. The land is part of me. I am vast because the land is spacious. It would kill me if our land became another strip mall or a convenience store where people stop to buy things that aren't good for them."

I thought about the crumpled bag of chips I had left on my passenger seat. I had promised Mama that I would take better care of myself, and I meant it. I had also talked to Ainsley about my health history. That morning, Ainsley had made something called, "Fakin Bacon" and an egg white omelet for me. It was so good that – despite the bag of chips that I had eaten for lunch – that I could almost smack my lips and re-taste my breakfast. Equally delicious was the fact that Ainsley (who had an unusually healthy family history) wanted to help me stay healthy so that we could be together for a long time.

Mama had a point. I understood what she meant. She was giving me permission to change.

"I understand what you are telling me, Mama. If I'm not happy anymore – and I'm not – then it's time for me to stop crying and change. But change is hard. I understand now why people don't want to change. They must feel secure doing the same thing they always did. There's a constancy about it. Doing the same thing feels safe even if it's no longer working."

Mama just nodded and said simply, "One thing leads to another."

"That's true," I replied. "The way we've always done things can lead to change. But change is unknown and that's scary to most people, including me. I'd rather hang onto the past and do what no longer works for me – just go through the motions – than to change and go into the unknown."

"That's true," replied Mama softly. "Whether we change or not, we don't know what is going to happen next."

Chapter Eighteen

I'll never forget when Spice came back to the pasture. I was so excited to see her that I barely acknowledged Sunflower who was leading her down the hill, murmuring to her as she held her hand under Spice's mouth. I hadn't been sure about how I felt about Sunflower. She didn't seem to be changing. The last time that I looked in her window, she seemed to still be eating the flesh of my friends – even though the housecat didn't appear that interested.

Plus, Sunflower *was* the farmer. That meant the decision to send us away ultimately rested on her. In many ways, I couldn't trust her or her kind. Humans ate animals. Everyone knew that. We cows eat only grass and grain. We are peaceful creatures. We don't hide ham sandwiches in our pockets and go around insulting other cows or any other beings – for the most part. How can you trust someone who might eat you or profit from your slaughter? But I forgot all of that when I saw Spice come back to the pasture. I was deeply grateful to Sunflower for nursing Spice back to health.

I lifted my head as they came close. Then Sunflower turned away and walked back up the hill. Spice touched her nose to my nose in greeting. When she touched me, the whole of our childhood came spiraling back. First, we were calves sprawled in sweet-smelling hay. The hay was so fragrant that I could smell it forever. The hay was so sweet that I didn't want to leave. But my spindly legs had other ideas. I walked around and around the stall that had enclosed us. We were both so young when they separated us from our mothers that neither of us remembered our mothers. We both had a sadness that penetrated deep inside of us. But we had each other. For as long as I could remember, I had been with my friend.

Then we grew too large for the stall. That's what I overheard a farmhand say. I would've been happy to continue to sleep in the sweet-smelling hay. But no one asked us what we wanted. The farmhands put us right next to each other outside in our separate caged-in areas. I had been entranced by the endless baby-blue sky. Then on another day, it was gray. Water poured down. At first, it was fun. I lifted my head. Streams of cool, refreshing water washed out my ears. But then my eyes began to sting. So, I went into the plastic hut and lay down in the straw that had been thrown on top of the gravel. I could feel the gravel through the straw. Hard and cool rocks made indentations on my soft warm belly. I heard rustling in the plastic hut next to me as my friend turned around to make herself comfortable. Knowing my friend was next door gave me comfort.

We grew up next to each other. Before we knew it, we were moved to the barn and went to the pasture every day with the others. We got pregnant the same month after a few years, gave birth the same month, and started producing milk. We were separated in the barn but could stand next to each other in the pasture where we talked about our lives. We were herded into the barn several times a day to be milked. When the uncomfortable machine chugged and sucked, it was only bearable because I knew that my friend was going through the same thing.

Sure, we squabbled – like the time recently when we were in the pasture and I temporarily chose Sunflower as my best friend, over Spice. I still don't know what I was thinking! That we argued just showed we meant something to each other.

The day we were reunited in the pasture, I closed my eyes as I nuzzled Spice. Her nose was soft and warm against mine. It was moist. I could sense she also felt the memories of her entire life flooding back. We had shared our lives. We were part of each other.

At first, I was content to stand next to her and swat flies off my sides with my tail. As far as I could tell that's why my tail was there. From time to time, I felt a touch on my side as her tail touched me as it made its way to swat a fly resting on her side. The sky above us was a blue dome. The grass under us was green. It smelled sweet. It turned into waves that rippled in the distance. The ground under our hooves was solid.

I felt well-being radiating out from her.

It felt like we could stand here forever.

"I've missed you," I said softly. "I was worried about you."

"I dreamed of you," she mooed softly. "We were playing in the pasture."

"I had the same dream," I marveled.

She told me she was tired and went to lie down in some nearby shade.

I watched her get settled down and then wandered off. At first, I wanted to hang onto the contentment being with Spice had brought me. I had been worried about her and then she came and stood next to me.

Now, without her by my side, I began worrying again. Would they let her rest without making her go to the barn to be milked? The nice farmhand was on duty today and it seemed like he would understand she still needed extra rest. Then I began thinking about the future.

I know, I know. Worrying about the future is never a good thing, but I couldn't help myself. What would happen to us in a year or two, when we stopped producing milk? It no longer brought comfort to me that we would probably be sent away together.

I felt agitated.

I walked toward a cow that I recognized. I remembered that she had a sour temper, but that didn't matter so much to me at that precise moment. I just wanted to not be alone. Any company was better than none.

We greeted each other and when the other cow asked how I was, I decided to be honest.

"I'm not sure," I answered. "I was really happy that my good friend who was sick, got better, and was released back into the pasture…"

"She's *your* friend?"

I nodded.

The tone in this cow's voice reminded me of why I usually keep my distance.

"I would be careful around her. She might be just pretending that she feels better. She might infect the entire herd. In fact, she may have already infected you."

Her nostrils quivered as she took a step back from me.

I felt myself bristling.

"I can assure you my friend did not infect me," I retorted. "The farmer took good care of her and I'm sure she didn't release my friend back to the pasture before she was all better."

I wasn't even going to bother to tell this cow that my friend had a name. *Spice.* I'm sure she would have something negative to say about that.

"Hmmm," replied the cow. Then she quickly asked, "What did your friend do?"

"What do you mean?"

"You know. What did she do to make herself sick?"

"It wasn't her fault," I said, quickly coming to my friend's defense. "She just got sick."

"That's what you say," replied the cow, keeping a skeptical-looking eye on me while lowering her head so she could sniff the grass. "But everyone knows differently. If anyone gets sick, it's because of something they did."

I batted my eyes innocently.

"Whatever do you mean?"

She raised her head and snorted. Then she hooved the ground with her front right leg and said, "You know what I mean. What did she do? Did she eat sour grass on purpose? Did she knowingly eat the wrong kind of clover, the kind that makes us bloat?"

"I can assure you that she did no such thing. She DID NOT make herself sick," I replied.

I could feel myself getting defensive. Who did this cow think she was? She was maligning my friend.

"Are you sure?" This cow certainly was persistent.

"She may have done something, but it wasn't on purpose," I conceded.

"I just asked because lots of cows make themselves sick on purpose because they can't stand the thought of being sent away." The other cow looked at me sadly.

"Oh," I said. I thought she was going somewhere else with this.

"As far as I know," I continued. "It wasn't on purpose. At least she didn't tell me anything to make me think that she planned it. But now that you mention it, I am feeling a little uncertain about the future. What's the point of my friend getting better if we're only going to be sent away in a few years?"

"Hmmph," snorted the cow.

She was older than me by about a year. It occurred to me that she would be sent away before us and might not want to talk about it.

"If you ask me," she replied, "we should be HAPPY to see others sent away."

"HAPPY?" I replied, incredulously. My jaw dropped. "What do you mean?"

"I meant what I said. HAPPY," she reiterated. We should be happy that someone else is being sent away and not us."

"But it will be us in a few years," I replied.

"BUT IT'S NOT US NOW," she retorted.

"You're kidding," I replied.

"NO, I'M NOT. How could I joke about such a thing?!"

"I don't know. I wouldn't kid about it." I saw an interesting-looking chicory flower growing near the fence and made a mental note to devour it later when I was alone. I didn't want to share it. For some reason, this conversation was making me feel very hungry and more than a little selfish. I was aware that I wanted the lavender blue petals of the succulent chicory flower all to myself. I didn't even think of bringing the flower to my recovering friend.

"Think about it," replied the cow as she eyed a tuft of longish grass. I imagined she was looking for things to eat later just as I was. "Who knows what is going to happen in a year. The world could end as far as we know."

She had a point. I was silent for a moment.

"You may be right," I replied finally. "But I would never be HAPPY about someone else being sent away."

"Why not?" she shrugged her shoulders.

"Why not?!" I replied.

"Is there a reason you keep repeating what I say?"

I didn't dignify her question with a response. I just stood perfectly still, except for my tail which switched from side to side.

"For one thing, their bad luck is your good fortune," she replied, swatting a fly nonchalantly with her tail.

"But I feel bad for them," I replied.

I felt prim. Almost against my will, my four knees tightened, and I stood taller. I felt my sphincter tightening. My voice became higher.

"It's bad manners to take happiness in someone else's misfortune."

"Bad manners!? I never heard of such a thing. Cows don't have manners!" she snorted. "Next, you'll be telling me that you're friendly with the farmer!"

I was indebted to Sunflower for saving the life of my friend. But I wasn't about to tell this cow that. She'd accuse me of preferring humans to my own kind. At that moment I did prefer humans – at least the farmer and the nice farmhand – to one of my kind. I knew I had to get away from this cow. She might be in denial about her own future, but she was also toxic. Before I walked away, there was one last thing I had to say to her.

"Cows can have manners too," I retorted. Then without pausing I added, "I have to go now. It was good talking to you."

I told myself that I wasn't really lying. Well ... maybe I was telling a white lie to make her feel better about herself. That was better than admitting to myself that I was telling a whopper. I really was just being polite.

I had walked away until I was sufficiently out of earshot. I looked for some long grass to graze on. When I turned around, I saw that she had walked in the other direction. As if she could see behind her, her tail switched.

If I could have bent over and thrown a cow pie at her, I would have.

I went back to grazing for a while then turned around. Her hindquarters were still facing me. I heard a distant, "toot, toot, toot."

At least I'm too far away to smell her farts, I thought. I had the uncharitable thought that her tooting was probably her way of having the last word.

I don't care, I thought.

Then I went over and devoured the chicory flower in one gulp.

It was unlike me to feel so irritated. I wanted to go over to my friend, who was still resting in the shade, and tell her everything. I felt rather meanspirited. I knew that my spiteful anger would be too much for my friend who was just getting better.

So, instead, I just stood near the wooden fence, after I ate the flower. I breathed in and out until I had exhaled all the anger that was inside of me.

Chapter Nineteen

I had meant to take a longer walk that morning. I wanted to create new habits and had read if you could do something new for thirty days then you could keep doing it indefinitely. I'd planned on walking for at least a half hour in the morning. But I had thought it would be a cooler day. With my bare hand, I wiped sweat from my brow. I wore my long-sleeved cornflower blue cotton knit top and my medium-weight charcoal sweatpants. Maybe I was overdressed. Even though it was still morning, I could feel the humidity rising. Or was the sweat from the short walk I had taken already? I decided that my uncomfortableness was probably due to both.

I stopped near the herb garden and stooped down to admire a patch of dill. With the morning dew sparkling on the feathery leaves, it looked like a magical forest. I plucked some of the green strands, pressed them to my nostrils, and inhaled. The soft wiry strands smelled enticing. I imagined the color green had a scent. I visualized deliciousness born on the wind. The wind felt green. I put the dill in my mouth. My taste buds came alive. As I savored the distinctive taste – a green zest with bitter undertones

— I was reminded of something that I had eaten recently. But I couldn't remember what.

I started walking again. There was a slight incline of a hill. I huffed and puffed. As I walked, I felt the humidity pressing down on me. Summer might be almost over, but it was still here. Cicadas hummed. The air pressed down oppressively like a damp cloth.

I thought about running errands and stopping at the convenience store to pick up a bag of chips. Then it came to me. That's where I remembered the flavor from. After I had visited my mother, I was feeling blue. So, I stopped at the store again on the way home and picked up another bag of chips. These chips were smooth, not ridged, and they were seasoned with dill. I told myself that at least I was consuming a vegetable. I smacked my lips and remembered how good the chips had tasted.

My feet began to hurt. What was I thinking that I would start my day by walking? I could look in the mirror and see that I was too heavy. Maybe I should lose weight before I started walking.

Then I thought again. Maybe I was being too hard on myself. Perhaps I looked better when I was heavier. I imagined myself as a large abundant goddess. I envisioned myself as wide as the land and as tall as the sky. Perhaps the land and the sky had sprung from me. My feet began to throb. Maybe I needed new sneakers, but I couldn't afford them. I could barely afford to pay

I stood outside the wooden fence and looked down at the pasture. I thought I spotted Cinnamon. She had a slightly odd body shape. She was longer and less wide than the other cows. Her brown color was easier to spot since most of the cows were black and white Holsteins.

"Cinnamon," I called. "Spice."

Cinnamon came trotting over. Spice, a darker shade of brown, was behind her.

I was touched when the two cows came running toward me. I had heard from Bob, the farmhand who I wasn't happy with, that Cinnamon, (he called her number fifty-five) balked and went in the opposite direction when it was milking time. Jimmy, the other farmhand, had told me that Bob didn't pull his weight. In particular, Jimmy had told me Bob didn't clean the barn when it was his turn. I had talked to Bob, and he said he would do better. Then he told me that he really needed this job, because he was taking care of his elderly mother in the trailer park where they lived on the far end of town.

I felt for Bob. After he told me about his mother, I always asked about her. When I first asked, he acted surprised. I told myself that he wasn't used to an employer asking about his life. But I don't think that he ever cleaned the barn again – at least not according to Jimmy.

At first, when I heard about Bob not doing his work, I was ready to fire him. But after he told me that he was taking care of his elderly mother, I couldn't let him go. Looking back, I see this was a sign I wasn't the type of person who could deal with having employees. Plus, I realized later he might have made up the story to manipulate me. I never heard of his elderly mother from any of the local people who stopped at the vegetable stand. I also never heard of her through anyone at church – even when I asked key people in the congregation. If there was someone in the community who was old and sick and needed help, they seemed to know about it.

Cinnamon and Spice took turns poking their heads through the wooden fence and nuzzling my hands. I loved each one of them up the way I always did. First, I patted Cinnamon's nose above her large and dark wet nostrils and stroked her between the eyes just the way she liked it. Then I petted the sides of Spice's face the way she liked it. I told each of them that I loved them and would not let anything happen to them.

I hoped I could keep my promise.

I wished I could afford to stop sending away the cows immediately. There was another batch of cows scheduled to be sent away in a month or so. I had the contract but hadn't signed it yet. In my fantasy, the cows and I would live together forever – or at least the cows would be able to live out their natural life spans while I could miraculously keep feeding them.

I felt bad I hadn't brought any slices of apples or cubed potatoes to give to the girls as treats. I wondered if they expected me to have treats now when they saw me.

Thinking of food made me hungry. Time had passed. The shadows were almost nonexistent now that the sun was straight up in the sky. It was time for lunch.

The next day, I set out again for my morning walk. I told myself that it was another day. It was. Perhaps that is how change is made – one step at a time. But first, you must have hope that change is possible. You can do it if you think you can. If you think you can't do it, then you won't. It's that simple.

I admired the farm as I walked. When my feet started to hurt, I pushed away the pain with the thought that Papa would be proud of me for keeping the farm running. But now I had Cinnamon and Spice in my life, too. Even though I loved them and wanted to protect them, I had to do what was necessary to keep the farm. Cinnamon and Spice would have to take a back seat for now.

For lunch yesterday, Ainsley had made me a curried dish of "cauliflower rice" – something they sold in the stores now – which is essentially cauliflower that was chopped up fine in the shape of rice. Ainsley mixed it with chickpeas, canned mushrooms, and raisins. It was yummy! Afterward, I opened my mail and went through my bank statement. With a sinking heart,

I realized that I needed to continue the contract. The farm's taxes were due soon and if I didn't pay them, I would lose the land.

Ainsley had been right about being included in the next round of layoffs, so I couldn't borrow money again. At least, I felt like I couldn't ask. Ainsley was collecting unemployment and was confident about getting something soon. But I had heard a lot of complaining about the job – before the threat of layoffs. I sensed that Ainsley didn't like being a lawyer.

Ainsley loved cooking, in general, and, in particular, enjoyed cooking for me. I, in turn, loved Ainsley's cooking. Lately, Ainsley has been cooking some very healthy and tasty meals. Just last night, we had vegan mac and cheese – made with tahini sauce (ground-up sesame seeds) instead of cheese and large mushrooms. I had to admit that If I didn't do something about my health, I wouldn't be able to keep the farm going. Ainsley had pointed out that everything –including the existence of Cinnamon and Spice – depended on me staying healthy.

I continued my walk. I felt guilty about having to send the cows away. I told myself that it wasn't rational for me to have named the cows. Cinnamon and Spice. Who did I think I was – the director of the Spice Girls? I used to sing along loudly to their hit single when I was alone in the pickup and the radio station played it. Then guess what happened? I met Ainsley. That was just what the Spice Girls were singing about – a lover who was your friend and how friendship lasts forever. Ainsley was just what I wanted – a friend, a lover, a mate, someone who cares for me every day.

I wondered if the Spice Girls would come and do a benefit for the cows. I may have named Spice for them subconsciously. Besides, didn't women and cows have something in common? Maybe there was something to the fact that women were called heifers, cows, and fat cows since biblical times. It's in the Bible. A woman at church told me. It made sense. Cows and women both have mammary glands, and we are designed to feed our young. Maybe that's why women are treated like cattle in some pornography like the large animal vet had said.

But as I walked past the pasture and toward the vegetable garden where the sunflowers beckoned, I thought, *the Spice Girls would never do a concert for my farm. Why would they? They probably get asked to do fundraisers all the time.*

Maybe I would win the lottery. Then I wouldn't have to worry about money.

But first, I would have to play the lottery.

I walked down the grassy tire tracks in the center of the garden, past the nutty-tasting arugula that was a great green to toss in salads past the green banana peppers, which I had just learned were full of vitamins, minerals, and other nutrients. I turned around at the end where I noticed some red tomatoes rotting into brown earth. I made a mental note to return with several baskets and salvage what I could. Then I walked up the small incline of the hill back towards the towering sunflowers.

Before I exited the garden, I passed the stands of catmint. Its clusters of heart-shaped leaves under its shoots of tiny lavender flowers shimmered in the morning light. Tangerine loved to rub catmint on his face when it was dried. It had to be dried and not fresh. I imagined that the cat must be interested in the texture of the crinkled leaves as well as the exotic and musky scent when I broke the leaves.

I tried to imagine my connection was only with plants and not with animals. Plants were fascinating. A plant often had medicinal properties as well as their uses for foods. Take catmint, for example. I heard that catmint was sometimes made into a tea for humans to cure insomnia.

I tried to imagine I had never connected with Cinnamon and Spice or with any of the cows. How easy life would be. How wonderful it would be to be oblivious to my health also. I could eat what I always had eaten. I could farm the way that I always had farmed. I could be a dairy farmer. I could keep the land as it always had been kept. But something nagged at me. What about my health? What about my aching feet? What about my uncle who just fell over one day, had a heart attack, and that was that? It was hard enough to keep things going when I was alive. But where would this farm be without me?

If only I didn't have any health problems. Maybe by ignoring them, I could make them go away. Not everyone knew their family history. Mama had reminded me of mine. What if she had never told me? What if I had gone somewhere else that day – maybe out to get a double scoop of chocolate ice cream on a sugar cone. Instead, I had visited Mama, listened to my family's health problems, and had equated my family's suffering to the suffering of the dairy cows being slaughtered after they were done being useful. Growing up on a dairy farm, it wasn't a stretch to equate people and animals. I was starting to pay more attention to my body and to trust how I felt. It had only been a few weeks since I gave up dairy, but already I felt better. I admit that I still craved ice cream – chocolate especially.

I began to think of miracles. If something was meant to be, then wouldn't it just happen?

In the Bible, Moses threw down his walking stick and the waters opened. He led his people out of slavery. I wanted to believe God had a plan. But maybe I was part of the plan. Maybe I was Moses, and the cows were my people.

I told myself the cows were not my people. For one thing, they weren't people. They were animals. I was an animal, too. But cows were a different species than me.

When I walked by the pasture, I made sure to keep my eyes straight ahead so I wouldn't look at any of the cows and so they wouldn't see me looking at them.

When I look back on that day, I see that I was acting like Queen Elizabeth I, hiding in the castle when her cousin Mary Queen of Scots was executed. Queen Elizabeth had ordered the execution. She had signed the order. But she must have felt guilty, guilty, guilty.

It may not be the 1500s, but I felt the same way.

I may not be eating beef anymore – or even dairy – but I was running a dairy farm even if I didn't plan to be around when the next batch of cows were taken away.

Chapter Twenty

I was standing in the pasture next to Spice when I spotted Sunflower striding by outside the wooden fence. I may have looked like I was staring straight ahead. But since I have eyes on the opposite sides of my face, I can see far more than most people think.

I spotted Sunflower rushing past the wooden fence of the pasture. She usually walks slowly. Ordinarily, she moves from side to side as she ambles toward the pasture. But that day was different. Her plump denim-clad thighs brushed each other more quickly and purposefully as if she had somewhere important to go. At first, I thought she was striding to see me – I mean us: me and Spice – but then I observed her going right past us. Maybe she was in her farmer mode and had some business to attend to.

Then I wondered, *was she avoiding me – and, if so, why?*

I thought of running up to the fence. There was still enough time to catch her. She walked briskly compared to her usual slow gait, but she still wasn't moving that fast.

No, I thought. *It has to be her idea to come to me.*

It felt like this thought came from the marrow of my bones. Maybe I was wise beyond my years because I only had another year or two before I was sent away. If I was killed before my time, did that make me older now?

Was older always wiser?

I hope Sunflower keeps her promise and doesn't have me and Cinnamon sent away, I thought. *But would she? Could she?*

I wondered what Sunflower was up to. I thought about sneaking out of the pasture and spying on her, but then thought better of it. If she was in a bad mood, I didn't want her to take it out on me. I had never seen her do this. But I knew to stay away from Ham Sandwich. I never knew when he was going to call me a "sneaky cow" or a "fat cow." I may be sneaky, but I wasn't fat by cow standards. Judging from the girth of Ham Sandwich, I suspected that projection may be at play. Or maybe this was just how humans acted. I didn't want to risk feeling the same way about Sunflower. Besides, I wanted to stay close to Spice to make sure she was okay.

Aside from the fact that I didn't want to give Sunflower the chance to show me that she was like the rest of the humans, intuition told me I had to wait for Sunflower to come to me. She had to realize I was here to help her. I didn't know how it worked, but I had a strong hunch she had to know that by helping me, she would be helping herself.

I didn't know how I was helping her – only that I was.

She knew where to find me when she was ready.

I went back to grazing on the tuft of onion grass growing near my front legs. Onion grass always made me gassy, and I would pay for this later. But at least I knew what to expect.

About a month later, I was lying down in my narrow spot in the barn and preparing to go to sleep. Suddenly I heard a commotion that could only mean one thing. The trucks had arrived and soon the barn would be emptied by almost half of the inhabitants. They always came at night. I closed my eyes tightly and prayed that Spice and I would be spared. I wanted all the cows to be safe. But I was so frightened when I heard the trucks that I thought of myself and my closest friend first.

I heard the human men shouting at each other and rousing the other cows by number. I heard the loud mooing that sounded an alert and meant "No. No. No."

Then I heard a cow screaming in a high pitch.

"Run, run," another cow bellowed. "Don't let them take you. Run, run. Hide – go anywhere but onto the truck. They're taking us to our death."

"I don't believe it," retorted another cow. "After all we've done for them."

my taxes. Who was I kidding? A goddess never had to worry about money.

Goddesses may get away with being large. But I was beyond large. I was as fat as a cow – no offense to cows. The cows didn't have a choice. We kept them penned in pastures and trapped in barns. How could they be in shape when we had bred them to eat large quantities of grass and grain engineered to be fattening?

Who was I to think I could change? I was lucky. Fate had been on my side. I was grateful that I had been able to keep the farm – so far. I hoped that I would be able to continue my good fortune. I knew that a lot depended on luck. I'd been lucky in the past. But how could a person continue to have good luck?

I made it as far as the wooden fence of the pasture. I stopped at the gate. I used to go in the pasture all the time, but now I hesitated. I told myself that it was my imagination, but I sensed the cows were angrier now. A cow could do a lot of damage with a head butt or a kick of one of her back legs. The cows seemed to be butting their heads more in the barn lately. Even though I okayed the chains that the farmhands put on their heads while they were being milked, I felt for the cows. Who could blame them? I wouldn't want to be hooked up to the milking machine and have chains put on me when I objected. Who wouldn't be difficult in that situation?

"Maybe it's not that bad. Perhaps they're just taking us to another farm, another pasture. We don't know where they're taking us. Maybe it's somewhere pleasant. Somewhere pleasant," said another cow, her voice trailing off. She sounded like she was trying to reassure us and herself.

It sounded like this cow was reassuring herself that humans would never do such harm.

"Somewhere pleasant?!" bellowed another cow. "Don't believe it for a minute. When they're done with us, they send us away to be KILLED! There is no coming back from where we are going."

Wait a minute, I thought. *I know that voice.*

The voice was as stubborn as it was shrill – as insistent as it was indignant.

"Hey," the same voice shouted. "Where do you think you're taking me? I WON'T GO, I WON'T."

I could hear the voice fading away as the cow left the barn and as, I could only assume, boarded the truck with the other cows.

The voice was unmistakably the same as the slightly older and ornery cow I had talked with in the pasture the day that Spice came back.

I remembered what she had said that day in the pasture and tried to heed her advice.

I tried to be happy like she had advised me and as I heard the trucks roll away and the cows who were left behind, settle back down. I was greatly relieved that the truck men hadn't come for me. If I was spared – for now – then I knew Spice would be spared also because we were the same age.

But the feeling of "whew" is not the same thing as being happy.

I was not happy that the others were taken away. It wasn't only because I knew that meant in a year or two Spice and I would be sent away also – I was terrified of that. I felt bad for the ones who were taken away.

I was the opposite of happy. I was deeply saddened. I wasn't only saddened because humans were slaughtering and eating my kind. I was sad because it was bad for the humans too, but they didn't yet know it.

Participating in the slaughter of innocent beings is to take part in your own demise.

Someday soon the trucks would come for them, too.

Chapter Twenty-One

"Do you know what the ingredients in this are?" I asked the woman standing in front of me in line at the table in the basement after the church service.

The minister was back from his summer-long vacation. The service was good – by which I mean I wasn't bored. I sat behind a toddler perched backward on her father's lap who played peek-a-boo with me. Judging from the line at the table downstairs, the potluck afterward was the main event. This was why people came to church – to eat with each other and to share their favorite recipes. I suspected there was a fair amount of competition going on around me. When it came to competition, I was usually clueless. I didn't even care for sports. It wasn't that I disliked them. I just didn't see what the point was. Who cared who won?

But most other people who I met at church were into sports. Or else they just pretended they were because they thought everyone else was. Often, people assumed I was interested in sports. I knew from experience that saying that you didn't follow the team (whatever team the other person supported) was a real conversation-stopper. I suspected that the competition inherent in sports – of someone having to be the winner, requiring someone to be the loser – spilled over for many. They had to prove they were worthy by making a dish that was deemed as "good." It was in church that I heard about competitive cooking for the first time – at least competitive cooking not on a television show.

Some were comparing notes on how their dishes stacked up with others.

Lately, I found myself asking questions about the ingredients of food often. It wasn't a bad thing for me to stop and think before putting something in my mouth. Before, if I was hungry or not, I would just pop something in my mouth without thinking.

Suddenly, everything had changed. Since, I thought about where food came from, I also considered whether the food I was about to eat was good for me – or not. I also paid attention to whether the food in front of me was good for the planet and other living beings. Candace had called it "mindful eating."

I felt so good that I wanted to spread the word.

"I'm in the process of eliminating all animal products from my diet," I explained to this same woman who was heaping a serving of casserole onto her plate.

"Then you're in luck. There's no meat in this casserole – just eggs and cheese.

"I'll have to pass then," I said. "I don't eat eggs or cheese either."

I didn't feel like explaining that eggs and cheese were animal products also. Besides, the woman in line who I was talking to had just taken a serving and might take offense.

"Hmmm," she commented. "A dairy farmer who doesn't eat cheese. I never heard of such a thing."

"Well, you've finally met one," I said. "Not eating meat wasn't hard for me to do, because I never really liked it. But I used to love eating cheese and ice cream. I loved it so much my doctor told me that I would probably lose weight not eating dairy – since it is full of saturated fat – and that the weight loss would help my feet."

"Oh," the woman said, "I didn't know that you were having problems with your feet. I hope you feel better," – as she spoke, she looked at me intently – "I'll be sure to bring something you can eat next time. There's some rice and beans you can eat further up the table." She pointed to a half-full Corning Ware bowl in front of us. The dish was white and tall enough to be considered deep. It had blue flowers on the side. The flowers looked like daisies, but I thought they were intended to be cornflowers.

CINNAMON: A dairy cow's (and her farmer's) path to freedom

I saw this woman almost every week, but I didn't know her that well. I was surprised by her compassion. She looked like a Holstein cow with her fluffy dark hair and her pale skin. She was heavy with broad cheeks and a high forehead. Her eyebrows jutted out, framing her face. She looked familiar. There was something about her large dark nostrils that looked like they could easily flare. I wouldn't want to be around her when got her dander up. She looked like she ate a lot of beef. But she looked like she consumed more cheese. Her big brown eyes slowly blinked, and I realized that there was also something docile and caring about her – like a cow.

"I was having problems with my feet also," said a tall older man across the table from me.

I looked up into his face. He was about a head taller than me. He wore silver wire-rimmed glasses and the top of the frames glinted under the fluorescent lights of the church basement.

"I had problems walking and had a pain in my heel. As it turned out, the diagnosis was plantar fasciitis. The doctor gave me a shot of cortisone, and the pain vanished." As he finished talking, the man whose name I didn't know heaped a generous serving of casserole onto his paper plate.

"The first thing my doctor suggested was a shot of cortisone," I told the man. "But then he told me it only lasts from six weeks to six months. He also told me the shot doesn't work on everyone and, even if it does, there are lots of negative side effects."

The man held the serving spoon in mid-air and looked at me oddly.

It looked like I had just burst his bubble about his 'miracle' treatment. His doctor had told him that there was a cure and apparently had not told him the rest. Maybe my fellow churchgoer wanted to believe in a magical solution. I thought of myself the day I had wished that I could do nothing, and things could stay the same.

"I mean I hope that the shot works for you – and I'm sure it will," I replied.

When I look back, I see I was just saying the kind of thing church people say.

The man seemed to relax. He smiled and looked at the next dish with relish. I almost envied his belief in modern medicine, except that I didn't think that much of most traditional doctors. It was obvious to me – as they scooted around town in their sports cars – that they were in it for the money. They were paid well for telling their patients what they wanted to hear.

"It's just that there are other ways of curing things," I replied. "My doctor told me that first before he gave me the shot, he wanted me to do the stretching exercises that he gave me –

which seemed simple. Then he told me if I lost weight, it would help my foot feel better."

The doctor had told me losing weight would make me feel better overall. Then he had given me a meaningful look. My doctor was one of the good ones. He probably was rare. He was a decent person. His Prius was parked directly in front of his small group practice. He had told me once that he cared about the planet and that he tried to "walk the talk," so he bought a hybrid car. It felt to me he sincerely cared about his patients and that he genuinely cared about me. He was telling me gently that if I lost weight, I would feel better.

"Good thing for me, I don't have to lose weight," retorted the man I had been talking to. He spoke over his shoulder as he darted ahead in the line toward the blue plastic Tupperware bowl of franks and beans. There was an indentation on the circular rim of the bowl where a lid could be snapped.

I looked at his broad back critically. He wasn't what someone who was being crass would call 'fat.' But he wasn't skinny either by any means. He was substantial. His weight looked like it fit him. I would be happy to drop some weight and look that way myself. But still... Perhaps it would help him if he lost weight, but his doctor let him think that by telling him that all he had to do to eliminate pain from his life was to get a shot.

I let his comment and my thoughts pass. He may just have made the comment to get back at me. There he was thinking he was set for life with his cortisone shot and then I came along bursting his bubble.

I let my thoughts go about his size. Who was I to judge? Everyone had their own size that worked for them. My size wasn't working for me. That's why I felt lethargic – kind of like I was moving under Jell-O.

I suddenly felt bad about focusing solely on myself. I was primarily eating differently because I had developed a friendship with Cinnamon and her friend Spice. But I was afraid to tell people. They might think I was crazy. I wondered about the woman who was compassionate toward me. Would she be compassionate to the cows too? What about the sheep and the pigs?

Even though I was a dairy farmer, I felt like it wasn't fair the cows were sent away to slaughter after their prime milking years. It wasn't fair for any animal to be treated cruelly just so we could eat them.

I didn't know where I could start having this conversation about how I felt about the animals. When I told my friend Candace that I had stopped eating red meat and dairy, she told me that chickens and turkeys were treated cruelly too. Then she told me that fish and seafood could feel pain and that they suffered also. We were having dinner at her favorite restaurant, and I had just ordered seafood linguini. She told me that fish farming was bad for the planet and that the oceans would soon expire in their capacity to be farmed but no one talked about it. We were having dinner at her favorite restaurant. She had ordered a cobb salad – "hold the gorgonzola, hold the bacon," she told the waiter – and was apparently feeling holier-than-thou. I ignored her comment, dismissing it as rudeness. Apparently, no one had ever told her you shouldn't insult someone's food while they were eating. It was because of Candace that I knew that passing judgement on what people ate especially when they were eating, was not the answer. I knew it didn't feel good to be criticized, especially when I was eating or about to eat. I also knew that it wouldn't help me to become the critical one. Criticizing others or being critical felt like the same thing.

    I moved forward in line, spooning a serving of white rice and red beans onto my plate. I spotted some tasty-looking green beans which I helped myself to. Then I took several helpings from a couscous and lima bean dish that looked like it didn't contain meat or dairy. There was enough food that I could eat. It was just a matter of changing my habits and thinking first. A bowl full of berries which I had picked up from the supermarket on my way to church sat on a side table with the desserts. If there was still some left later, I would have some of the berries for dessert.

    Aside from the long table that was laden with food, there were smaller card tables with plastic tablecloths of different colors set up in the basement. Most of them already had people sitting at them.

Then I sat down at an empty table covered with a cherry red tablecloth. Harry, a dark-skinned middle-aged man, whom I had spoken with before, came and sat next to me. I first met Harry at the library on Main Street where he was a librarian. I was looking for some books on wildflowers, and Harry found some good books for me. At the table in the church basement, Harry started asking me if the books were helpful for me and then he mentioned he raised African violets, that he had a large collection of them in his home, and that he had just returned from an African violet convention in Chicago.

I expressed surprise that there was such a convention and told him that I loved African violets. The conversation progressed from there to roses, especially pink ones which seemed to bloom more readily. Then he mentioned a nearby restaurant that had just announced that it was closing. He told me that he had never particularly liked the food, except for the pork chops.

"They're pretty good," he told me.

I could tell by his radiant smile that he loved pork chops.

I thought about the hog that I had sold and said nothing. I felt so guilty about selling the pig that I might have flinched. I had the hog since he was a cute little pink piglet with innocent eyes and a curly tail. I had never named him, but every time someone mentioned ham, pork, bacon, or sausage, I thought of the hog that I had sold.

Then Harry added that he was sorry to see the restaurant go even if he had never liked the food. I agreed but told him that I could no longer eat what they served anyway since they served mostly animal products and I had changed my diet.

I purposely didn't tell him that I hardly went to any restaurants because I couldn't afford to eat out that often. I didn't want to act like I felt deprived because I couldn't afford to eat out that much. I knew that I was lucky. I had my farm and I had Ainsley. And I still had Mama then. I was very lucky in a world where so many were suffering. And I didn't mention the fancy restaurant where I went with Candace, where she treated me, because that felt like bragging.

When I told him that my goal was to become vegan, Harry stiffened a little and looked uncomfortable. The friendliness on his face was replaced with apprehension. His eyes narrowed. Harry was slender and had good posture. He sat up even straighter.

He looked as though he was waiting for me to say something critical about him eating pork chops. Then I added that I wasn't totally vegan yet and was changing gradually. He shifted in his seat and appeared to relax.

That reminded me of something Candace had said to me the evening when I told her that I was changing my diet and was no longer eating beef, pork, or dairy. She had told me I could expect to find that people were very defensive about what they ate – especially when it was meat. She said this was because the cells of their bodies were created by the food they ate. She then explained the people who were defensive weren't bad people. It's just that their bodies became defensive because they felt like they were defending themselves. Later, I thought this made sense. In a way the people were defending themselves – even if they would be better off with a plant-based diet. I thought about the fact that people's bodies were made from what they ate. When I had talked with Candace, she said, "Change is hard." This comment was made in one of Candace's wise moments which weren't that rare. She also said that people suppressed their feelings about eating animals and often felt guilty.

I wasn't judging Harry when he mentioned that he loved pork chops.

I was quiet and maybe I flinched because I was feeling guilty about selling the hog. I had felt bad at the time. But I hadn't made the connection about loving the hog and eating pork – especially bacon. I didn't stop eating bacon until after I had promised Mama I would take better care of myself. Everyone knew what bacon does to your arteries.

So, I wasn't judging Harry about eating pork.

I was judging myself.

Chapter Twenty-Two

The sky was gray as I stood in the field thinking profound thoughts. I'd like to be able to tell you the sky was clear and blue. Everybody always likes blue skies, right? Sunny days appear beautiful and tranquil. It's hard to imagine anything bad could happen under perfect skies. Blue skies seem like they will last forever. But I don't need to tell you sunny skies don't last forever and that bad things do happen under them.

I tried to keep my thoughts sunny, but I could no longer deny what's happening. Clouds had gathered, and the sky was gray. It was the kind of gray that seems like it could last forever. It was dreary and depressing. It looked endless like the clouds would never move. It made me wonder if there were storm clouds in my future.

I felt a rumbling in one of my stomachs.

Uh oh, I thought.

I moved away from my friend Spice and discreetly farted. Excuse me, rather I had some cow flatulence. I thought the fart was my secret, but Spice moved a good bit away from me.

"Phew," I heard her say.

"Phew yourself," I replied.

She was all better, and it was nice to have her back in the pasture – even if we were past the nuzzling stage and had moved on to arguing about farts. It was nice to have someone to argue with in the pasture – someone who I loved and knew I would still be friends with after our argument and for forever, as long as that would be. That's what I was wondering about. Change. Specifically, what the possibilities were that change might happen before we were scheduled to be sent away.

I felt another rumbling – this time in another section of my middle.

"PFFFTTT."

There was nothing discreet about this. I had let it rip. The fart echoed across the field. There was nothing pastoral about it. People just see a beautiful scene when they pass a pasture. They don't imagine flatulence riding the wind.

Just then, a couple of people walked close to the fence and one of them mooed at us. I really didn't know what to make of that. Who did he or she or they think he or she or they was –mooing at us so familiarly? None of them knew us. They weren't the humans who brought us snacks and petted our noses.

I felt a rumble in one of my stomachs, so I turned my back to them and farted. Then I switched my tail because I was irritated.

Who were these people? What were they doing near our pasture? Given the familiarity – the complete lack of manners – I felt justified in farting in their direction.

The humans noticed I had turned around and had swished my tail in irritation. I heard them behind me as they laughed and said I looked irritated. I was! I stalked off to the other end of the pasture where I could graze in peace. I turned my head to call Spice, but she was already at my side. I guess she didn't like the humans either. She probably was also glad to get away from the stink cloud of my fart, which hovered in the air behind me.

"I hope you got it all out," was all she said.

Like you never fart, I thought to myself crossly. But I knew I would never get the last word in, so I didn't say anything. I just let her think she won.

When we got to the other side of the pasture, near the line of the deciduous trees where I had escaped one day long ago, we turned around. The humans were long gone. I guess they continued their walk – maybe they were afraid of storm clouds also.

I stood next to Spice in silent contentment. Whenever I worried about the future, I just took a deep breath and exhaled. I didn't want to make Spice anxious because I knew fretting wasn't good for her. I don't know what she heard in the barn when the trucks came to take the older cows away. Now we were the older cows. It felt strange thinking that we were the next to go. The thought made me feel jittery all over. I felt my intestines contracting like I had to poop. But then, the feeling passed.

Anxiety is contagious. If I made Spice more anxious then she would escalate my jitters. So, I didn't say anything. For all I know, she might be having the same thoughts. Maybe she was sparing me. We stood there in companionable silence.

What else could we do?

We could make platitudes to make each other feel better, but it didn't feel good to lie. We could've said things like, "Tomorrow may never come," or "Maybe things will finally change." But the sun has a habit of rising and setting – even though it feels like a miracle. Change may be a necessity, but you know the saying, "the more things change, the more they stay the same."

I wondered if change was possible. Spice turned back around and faced the back fence marked by the line of leafy trees behind it.

There I was under endless gray. A passerby might have thought I was looking out over the pasture. Even though I could never be tired of gazing at the land that I loved, I was lost in my thoughts.

Change was part of life. Every day was different. Despite that we were on a schedule – that we slept in the barn and had to go back to the barn at regular intervals to be hooked up to the milking machines – each day was different.

On some days, the sun rose in an artic blue sky. Other days were cloudy and overcast. That was different. Other days were rainy. Sometimes the rain was soft and constant like a gentle shower. Some days it rained heavily, and the downpour made me run for cover.

Once there was heat lightening in the distance. Other times, the lightening seemed to come straight down, the crack of thunder so loud that it made me jump and run for the barn – which seemed like a place of safety and not just the smelly residence where they housed us. That was very different.

Change was happening all around us, and it was out of our control. Maybe that's why people resisted it. But if you didn't allow change to make you do things differently, then it could be dangerous. For instance, if I didn't allow the lightning to chase me into line to go back in the smelly barn, I might be hit by the next bolt.

I could resist change. I could say, "this too will pass" and try to stay in the pasture. But where would that leave me? I could run and hide under a stand of trees. Of course, the decision ultimately wouldn't be mine. One of the farmhands or both would decide it wasn't safe us to stay out in the storm and herd us back into the barn. If there were any ornery cows who wanted to stay in the pasture, they wouldn't have a choice. But to tell you the truth, I never met a cow who was that grouchy. We knew when the farmhands had our best interests at heart.

I thought of changing awareness. Wasn't that change, too? The cows seemed to be more aware of our predicaments. There was more eye rolling and more grumbling. Maybe communication between cows and humans could change. It seemed that Sunflower had understood me that day when I got her to let me out of the pasture. I got the impression that I had directed her behavior with my thoughts – even if she was acting crazy and looking at the sky. Maybe if I could keep her responding to my thoughts, then her awareness could change also.

Maybe if I could get her to understand me, then she could change things before Spice and I were sent away. I knew it was a long shot, but I had to try. I had to imagine a future where the trucks no longer came for us.

I wondered what the humans were up to. Far in the distance, I could see the cars flashing by on the highway. Smoke hung in the air and drifted into the pasture. I could smell their exhaust. It smelled like metal and rubber and burning garbage. It smelled like something else too – but I couldn't identify it.

They were driving by so quickly, that I doubted they even bothered to look toward the pasture to see us. I had an advantage because I was standing still. I could hear my thoughts. I didn't feel better or worse, just different.

Where were they going?

I saw flashing red lights and heard screaming at the intersection. It seemed like the humans were angry and in a hurry. They seemed to turn their anger on each other. I had seen this before. It was a sign of living in captivity.

I wondered what they were running from.

Was their exhaust the smell of fear?

It seemed like they were trying to escape from something.

I wondered what it was.

Maybe they were afraid of the same things that I was.

Chapter Twenty-Three

A triangle of yellow light fell through the upper right corner of the chapel window. A piece of the darker stained glass must have fallen out.

I was sitting in the front pew of the little chapel in the retirement home. The walls were bluish green like the sea. I felt like I was under water.

I held my head in my hands. Sitting next to me, Ainsley rubbed my neck. This consoling touch released a fresh wave of sobs from me.

"Kathrine lived a good life. She was a farmer's wife. She worked the farm. She was a steward of the land. She was a God-fearing woman who went to church."

I was still sobbing. Even so, I paused to turn my head, looked at Ainsley and rolled my eyes.

My Mama was not God-fearing, I thought to myself sarcastically. *And she did not go to church. Well, she did go but only when she felt like it – now and then.*

I had told the head of the home that my Mama was not religious. But the woman – an older woman with salt and pepper hair, a kind face, and pearl-gray rimmed reading glasses – told me gently she'd rather a minister conduct the service than a lay person. I suspected that lay person would be her. She seemed to be running everything. I wondered what it felt like knowing you were operating a retirement home where you might end up soon – if you could afford it. She seemed like a kind and caring woman. She seemed genuinely sad my Mama had died and so suddenly. The woman seemed like she had a lot on her plate, and I didn't want Mama's memorial service to be one more thing.

So, I said yes to having a minister do the service. I guess he couldn't help himself when he said she was a God-fearing woman. That was the type of thing you'd expect a minister to say. But then he went on to say that she was a caring woman, a leader, someone to look up to. He mentioned she was part of many clubs at the retirement home, had made friends quickly, and she would drop what she was doing to help others.

Someone must have told him about her, and he must have paid attention.

But there was a lot he left out. He didn't mention that she had once wanted to be a musician who played in an orchestra, but then Mama didn't talk about it. He didn't mention the fact Mama wore heels when she had been young but then in her forties swapped them for comfortable shoes. But he did say she had helped to manage the medical care for an older friend whom she had met in her book discussion group. I had barely known about the group and had never heard of the friend. Yet this friend – who for all I knew was still living and was sitting somewhere in the pews behind me – was someone Mama had made a difference too.

Mama had made a difference to me also by insisting that I take better care of myself. It had been more than a month since I had started walking every couple of days and since I had given up dairy and beef and pork. I had turkey, but only now and then. In the past month, I only had chicken once. I doubted I wouldn't have it again because I no longer liked the taste. I had once loved it. The jury was out on turkey and seafood. I liked both but rarely ate them. But I planned to give them up eventually too. I also had given up snacking on chips. I had lost a little weight – though I was still wearing the same clothes.

Even now, wearing my black short-sleeve blouse over my one pair of black pants, I could feel I was a little thinner as I sat on the hard pew. I was immensely sad, of course. I had never expected Mama to die so suddenly. I should have known because she had looked so weak the last time I saw her. It's just that she was my Mama. I had expected her to live forever.

It was strange to be so grief stricken but at the same time to be feeling so good overall. It seemed that not eating creatures that I loved – or the food made from their milk – agreed with me.

I felt alive in a new way that was hard to describe. The little bit of weight I lost so far was enough for my feet to feel better. Beyond that, I felt like I had a new body. I had felt lighter and happier before my Mama passed and I expected that I would go back to feeling good. If my cells were formed by the food I ate, and I was changing what I ate, then my cells were changing more than usual.

Even as I appreciated what the minister was saying about Mama – that she was a selfless woman and that she was an example that thinking of other's first was a virtue – I couldn't help thinking that maybe she should have thought of herself more. Just like my uncle, she had leaned over to pick up something on the floor – her linen napkin had fallen on the home's dining room floor – and died instantly. I knew that she had gone to the exercise club at this retirement home where they were known for their gourmet food. Their rich food was a major reason that many people came to live there. But maybe controlling your weight wasn't enough – even if you could still look good with clogged arteries.

When the doctor had called to tell me that Mama had died, he asked me if I wanted an autopsy performed on her, I immediately said "no." I didn't want her to be poked and probed. It was hard for me to comprehend that she had died. How could she be dead? She was just telling me she was looking forward to going to the mall. But, but, but. When I calmed down, the house doctor told me she probably had a massive heart attack and that she was not in pain. I came to the home to collect her belongings and afterwards was walking past the dining room when I was leaving. The staff person who had served Mama her last dinner told me proudly that Mama's last meal had been a main course of Filet Mignon with mashed potatoes and fresh green beans.

The heavyset waitress, who I recognized from when I used to have lunch with Mama, told me the appetizer had been bacon wrapped scallops. There was always dessert, of course. But since Mama usually didn't usually eat dessert, I didn't ask what it was. I don't know what got into me, but after I talked to the waitress, I flew into a rage and demanded to see the house doctor. I could tell from the deep timber of his voice that this was the same man who had called me to inform me of Mama's death. I told him what she had for her last meal. We looked at each other wordlessly. I broke the silence by accusing the home of killing Mama. Then I broke down into sobs. The doctor told me I was obviously distraught. He had me sit down in a shiny brown padded leather armchair in his office and summoned someone to get me a glass of water. He told me again that he was very sorry Mama had died. He mentioned Mama had been in excellent physical condition for her age and that he was shocked at her death. His eyes were red when he said this. I could tell that he was upset. His compassion calmed me down.

But now as I sat at the funeral service, I shook my head. Maybe it was her time. But the food she had for dinner probably hadn't helped.

Most likely she had eaten her appetizer and main course and then fell over dead.

It seemed like ministers always went on too long. This one was no exception. Maybe he was paid by the hour, I thought. I let the uncharitable thought go. The minister would die himself someday soon. Another minister would take his place. We were all going to die. I moved a little closer to Ainsley.

I wondered which of us would live longer. Then I banished the thought from my mind. I was practical but at the same time I knew there was no point in worrying about the future. All we had was the present moment. I was lucky to have to have such a great love as Ainsley.

Ainsley was my person.

But suddenly I felt very alone. My Papa had died, and my Mama had died. I was an only child. I had no cousins that I was in touch with. Ainsley was my everything. I had Cinnamon and Spice too – but would I be able to keep them?

They say that God sees everything. Did He see me the times when I walked by the pasture but couldn't look at it because I was afraid to see Cinnamon? I was afraid that I had told her a lie when I promised her that she and Spice would not be sent away.

Did God cause my Mama to die? Did I do something?

I banished the questions almost as soon as I thought it. I knew it wasn't fair of me to blame God. It was just Mama's time to go. That's what Candace would've said. Thinking of Candace, who had lost her parents when she was a child, made me grateful that I had had Mama for as long as I did.

The morning sun had shifted. It was higher in the sky. Rays fell through the panes of violet and gold. The light in the chapel was dimmer than when the small group of mourners had filed in earlier. All I heard of the minister's droning was the pauses.

The room seemed hushed.

The bronze urn full of my mother's ashes was on a pedestal at the front. She had requested her ashes be scattered behind the pasture, marked by the line of deciduous trees.

Some months after my Papa's death, she had told me that she wanted her ashes strewn with his among those trees. "We used to love watching the sun set over the line of trees," she had told me. In the autumn, it looked like the leaves were ablaze with the setting sun. Sometimes the birds sat in the tops of the trees at sunset, and they all seemed to fly away in a group. Their bird calls formed a giant shriek. Below them, everything was orange. Even the pasture, in front of the trees, closer to us, was tinted orange. The pasture with the forest behind us was all that we could see. The land seemed to go on forever."

The trees were part of a public park. I suspect that scattering ashes there was illegal but that's where my Papa was. Now my Mama would join him.

Some people would say I was an orphan now.

A few months later, I still felt the absence of my Mama and Papa acutely. Who was I without them? I had never wanted children – neither did Ainsley – but I knew from the couples at church who had young children, that parents tended to look ahead into the world their children would live in.

I didn't have younger siblings to care for, so I didn't relate to younger children. They weren't part of my world. I never wanted children because it was a desire I just didn't have. One time when Papa was asked if he cared about not having grandchildren, he replied, "You don't miss what you never had." That's how I felt.

I knew that if I remained childless, I could experience life in a way that I could never do if I had a child or children and had to put their needs first. But now that I was experiencing such anguish over losing my mother – my last living parent – I had a larger reason to be grateful that I didn't have children. I wouldn't be putting them through such anguish at losing me. I was reducing the amount of suffering in the world.

Not having children also meant that I tended to look back. I was connected to the farm because I was born there. I was honoring my parents. I was remembering my grandparents who had died when I was so little that I could barely remember them now. I was honoring the people I came from.

I had Cinnamon and Spice. I had talked about them so much that Ainsley had come to the pasture fence with me and brought bags of snacks for them – apple slices, cabbage leaves, and quartered carrots. I loved Cinnamon and Spice. They were like my children. I loved them as much as I loved Tangerine, our cat. And I would never send him away.

CINNAMON: A dairy cow's (and her farmer's) path to freedom

Chapter Twenty-Four

I was so bored. I swished my tail and gazed out over the pasture. If I had a watch strapped to one of my four legs, I would have checked it to see how much "free" time I had until it was time to be milked. I wished Spice would hurry up and come join me. I could see her in the distance peeing like a racehorse. She preferred urinating as she stood looking away from us, standing in the corner as if it were in private – as if the rest of us couldn't see her peeing in the pasture. She was facing in the direction where most of us were standing. A curtain of water came down from her hind quarters, blurring her udder.

She must have drunk a lot from the water fountain last night and then not have gone all night. There was a metal water fountain in between the slots where we slept. Two of us shared one fountain that we turned on by pressing a black lever with our noses. The cow who slept next to me didn't like to get up after she laid down for the night, so I didn't have any competition when I got up to get a drink.

The trough inside that ran against the wall was supposed to be filled with water. But it was usually left empty – especially when Ham Sandwich was on duty – so Spice may have drunk extra water from the fountain. Maybe she thought the water may run out.

Personally, I had no compunction about peeing in the gully of cement just in front of my stall where the farmhands would come in the morning. I had to get up, turn around, and stretch out to pee there, but it was worth it. I knew that the farmhand on duty would step in my river of pee and become so angry that he would curse. Then before he fed me with a bale of hay, he had to sweep up my urine and wash the area with a bucket of water. The hay got a little wet on the bottom, but I didn't care. When it was Ham Sandwich's job to feed me, I got an extra thrill out of him stepping in my puddle of pee. *That's what you get for calling me a "fat-cow"* I would think to myself. I called it cow-ma.

In the pasture, Spice finished peeing. Finally! She started sauntering over in my direction. When she came closer, I could see her beige nostrils, her long brown nose, and evenly spaced eyes. Her perky ears flapped in the wind. I was taller than her so I could even see the dark brown ridge of her spine travelling down her back. She moved a little faster as she approached me. It wasn't fast enough to be a run, but it was faster than her normal lumbering gait. You might call it skipping. As she skipped toward me, her belly swung from side to side in the wind.

I stood still in the muddy grass. Only my tail moved. It had rained the day before and it was cooler but still humid. The flies were out.

I saw the sun reflecting in Spice's shining brown eyes. Her eyes seemed to smile at me. I was her cow, her home, her safe place. I knew this now. I was the one. No one could love her more than me. I was so relieved we were the same age. That meant that we would never have to be apart until after we were sent away together. I was still apprehensive about the future. But the thought that we would face the future together gave me comfort.

I was her best friend. I was almost her everything until that other cow came along. Since my true best friend had become sick and had gotten better, I was so glad to have her back that I tolerated this other cow. She was Spice's friend too – even if I was Spice's BEST friend. However, since she was Spice's friend, that meant she was part of Spice too. When Spice was sick this cow and I had stood together in the field, sending our friend positive vibrations.

Fortunately, that other cow was somewhere else grazing. I had Spice all to myself.

I didn't move a muscle. I heard a rumbling coming from deep within me.

Uh Oh, I thought.

I wondered what was coming next.

I always was relieved when I saw my friend Spice coming. That meant she was safe. Maybe this time, I had gotten so relaxed that I was going to cut one loose. Who knew what was coming. I might drop a large cow pie behind me. I didn't want to do that as Spice came closer. She might skip off and play with that other cow.

So, I did what I rarely do. I held whatever the rumbling was about in. I clenched my sphincter and didn't move any other muscles. Spice joined me and sensed I didn't want to play. We stood together in companionable silence.

But because I was tensing my sphincter, I couldn't relax and enjoy the moment.

"Excuse me," I said.

Spice looked alarmed.

"What did you do?" she asked and gingerly sniffed the air.

"Nothing," I replied. "Yet."

She started to back up.

"I have to move away for a moment, but I'll be right back. Don't go anywhere."

"Ok," she replied.

I moved away a bit – out of smelling distance. Then I went a little further. When I relaxed my sphincter, I felt more than flatulence coming out of me.

Splat!

It felt like I had to go again. While I was waiting, I began to worry that Spice might be as bored as I was. I loved being in the pasture. But I knew that I would have to go back to the barn and be milked soon. Then I would have to go back again. Depending on who was on duty, we might have to go a third time. If it was Ham Sandwich's day, then he would do the bare minimum. Our udders might be full, but we would get away with only being milked twice. But we would still have to go back into that stinky barn to sleep.

So, it wasn't that being in the pasture bored me. It was our routine. I was tired of being milked several times a day and looking forward to nothing. I usually liked looking at the pasture and at the changes in the sky but every now and then I wondered if I was fooling myself. I knew we would sleep in the smelly barn and be sent away after a few years. What was the point?

I wondered if Spice felt the same way. But I couldn't ask without running the risk that the question would make her depressed. I loved being with her in the pasture, but it still got boring for me – and maybe for her also.

There was only so much we could do here. I could show her how I had once escaped through the gap in the back fence, which seemed like long ago. But she might want to go on an adventure, too. It was harder for two cows to escape together. We might be seen by some humans and get caught. I couldn't escape and leave Spice by herself in the field. Ever since she had gotten sick, I felt protective and wanted to be by her side. Besides, I didn't want her playing with that other cow.

Splat!

As my dung hit the ground again, I decided that I couldn't risk Spice getting as bored as I was. It wasn't enough to stand together in the pasture and argue over who farted last. I would have to elevate the conversation.

I wandered back to my place next to Spice's side and before she could ask me how it went, I said to her matter-of-factly, "Tell me what you know about money."

She blinked her big eyes in surprise. The fringe of her thick lashes seemed to lengthen.

"Money?" she asked. "What makes you ask about that?"

"I heard Sunflower talking about it one day," I replied. "I had never heard the word before, but it seemed important."

I didn't tell Spice that Sunflower had mentioned money in terms of having to borrow some to get Spice's illness treated. I didn't want to remind Spice that she had been ill. She had been doing so well lately. She was almost back to her old self, but I could tell that she was a little wobbly.

"'Sunflower?'"

"That's the name that I gave to the farmer. She named us so I thought I would name her."

Spice regarded me levelly and nodded.

"'Sunflower,' I like that. Maybe you were right when you said the farmer had a lot in common with us. I became close to her when I was sick. I heard her talk about money a few times. It seems like she is always worried about it."

Now it was my time to nod.

"Was she talking to you?" I asked, my tail flicking a fly from my side.

"Yes, she was. But I don't think she knew I understood her. Do you want to learn about money or not?"

I looked at her expectantly and held my long tongue.

"Well one time she – I mean Sunflower – was talking to me about money and another time, I heard her talking to one of the farm hands when she was on the way to come see me when I was still in quarantine."

"And?"

"I was just getting to it. Please be patient."

I wondered which farmhand, Spice overheard Sunflower talking too. But I didn't want to ask too many questions.

I inhaled deeply and exhaled. The air in the pasture smelled like us – like cows and cow dung. There was probably a little cow pee mixed into the scent. It also smelled like the fresh grass that had been planted there just for us. It smelled like home.

"When I overheard her talking to the farmhand, she mentioned that she couldn't pay him on time because the property taxes had gone up. The farmhand seemed to understand."

It must have been Jimmy, I thought. Ham Sandwich would never accept not being paid on time.

"Property taxes?!" I asked. "You mean they charge money to live here?"

Spice nodded.

"Money" – explained Spice – "is something that humans made up. Sometimes their self-worth is based on it – you know their self-importance."

I widened my eyes.

"I didn't know this," I replied.

"Well, now you do," retorted Spice. "When humans have more money, they feel superior to other humans who have less money."

This didn't make any sense to me. I couldn't hold my tongue any longer.

"Why would anyone want to feel superior to anyone else?"

"Don't be silly. There's always a pecking order – even among cows," Spice replied. "Not to mention the fact that we used to be money."

"Be money! Us!?" I could barely contain my curiosity.

She looked at me coolly and chewed her cud.

"I meant what I said," she said finally. "An old cow told me that in ancient times the kings valued their worth on how many cows they owned. They even invaded other lands and took the cows as their own. Haven't you ever heard the expression 'a cash cow'?"

I shook my head.

"I never heard of such an expression. It sounds ridiculous. We don't exist to make some king wealthy."

"That's right," said Spice. "I thought the same thing when I first heard the expression. Obviously, a human thought it up – not one of us."

We both stood for a moment in silence. We were tired of being defined by humans – of being mooed at and told we were cute and then being eaten for lunch.

We were silent for another moment that seemed like a very long time.

I really did not know what to say. But I did have one thing to say about our previous conversation. In fact, I couldn't help myself. I had almost interjected this when she was talking but held my tongue.

"Older," I corrected her.

"What?"

"Older not old. You said you heard this from an old cow. You should have said 'an older cow.' We never get to be old here."

Spice regarded me silently.

Once again, I had mentioned the unmentionable.

I looked back at her silently.

A long moment passed.

"Before you INTERRUPTED me, I was talking about the pecking order," emphasized Spice.

I widened my eyes in an attempt to look inquisitive.

Think about it," she explained. "The cows in the front of the line are rather bossy and peremptory."

"That's a pecking order?" I asked. "I thought that they were anxious because they knew they were going away next and were behaving strangely."

Oops. I had mentioned the future again. I hadn't meant to, but I guess it was inevitable since we were talking about a concept that was larger than just trading insults about our farts.

We were both silent again for a moment.

Spice was right. The cows in the front of line did act like thought they were better than us. I chose to ignore their behavior. Not everyone acts right, and I consider the bad behavior of others really to be about them. Some might say I don't know my place.

But I was aware something was going on now that made me feel bad. I was going to address it.

"Excuse me," I said. "You're treating me like I'm a little slow – like a sheep."

"See," Spice replied. "You do understand this. You think sheep are slow – so you feel superior to them."

"I don't think sheep are slow. I know they are not fast to catch on to things like we are. Everybody knows that. But I do not feel superior to them, I just know I am different. In fact, I don't feel superior – or for that matter inferior – to anyone. I don't have to because I am secure in who I am."

"Whatever," said Spice. "You said you wanted to learn about money. Do you want to hear what I have to say or not?"

I breathed in and out as I nodded. I felt more relaxed. I really did want to hear what Spice had to say.

"Before you INTERRUPTED me, I was going to say I do not think that Sunflower is one of the humans whose self-worth depends on money. She's too down to earth. But she's part of the system of money that humans created because she has to be. Money is a system of currency that humans exchange, but it affects us too. It allows us to stay here. Sunflower told me that she was afraid she might lose the farm because the property taxes had gone up."

I shook my head in amazement. I saw an orange butterfly flit by out of the corner of my eye. There must be some interesting flowers around here.

Spice gave me a stern look that snapped me back to attention.

"This land isn't free – even though it feels like the most natural thing in the world to us. It sounded to me that if it wasn't for Sunflower, this land wouldn't even be here. She has to pay money for lots of things. For instance, she has to pay the farmhands," she stated.

I knew half of that was a waste. But I just satisfied myself with a silent eye roll that Spice ignored.

"Even our food and the grass seed have to be paid for with money," added Spice.

"You're kidding me. That doesn't seem right," I replied. These things are necessary to our survival – like air. I took a breath and swatted some flies with my tail.

"Does she have to pay for the air, also?" I asked.

"Not that I know of," replied Spice. "But even water requires payment."

I nodded as I chewed my cud. Things were starting to make sense.

Chapter Twenty-Five

Ainsley knocked on the door of the ramshackle house. There was no answer.

"Looks like she's not there," shrugged Ainsley. "I forgot our bag of treats. I'm going back to the pickup."

The largest cow I have ever seen, stuck her head over the fence and mooed softly. I moved closer to the wooden fence and put my hand out to stroke her furry nose. We were about the same height. Her hair was longer than any of my cows. Its glossy sheen reflected the sun.

I had heard most cows would naturally have horns. Milking cows were dehorned at birth. I never did it. But when I was young, I once saw a farmhand take a saw and cut the horns off a spindly-legged heifer. I felt very sad and ran home to ask Papa why they did it. He replied that they did it because it always had been done.

Someone had forgotten to dehorn this cow when she was a calf, or maybe they thought it would be a novelty to have a cow with horns.

She turned sideways beside the fence. From her large brown eyes to the back of her hump midway down her spine, she was a dusty gray. She was white in the middle with a dusting of gray on the front of her two front legs and on the upper part of her muscular back legs. Then she was gray again toward her rump. On closer inspection, I noticed that the gray on her back flanks looked like the smatterings of an impressionistic painting. Her white coloring underneath came through in the star-like pattern of snowflakes.

"I see you found Beatrice, or maybe she found you," said a smiling woman with high cheekbones who came up behind me. She had short blunt cut sandy brown hair. The ends of her hair brushed the collar of her red and black checked flannel shirt. There was something arresting about her. She had the radiant look of someone who was at peace with herself.

"You must be Helga," I said, smiling back.

"Yes," replied Helga. "I'm sorry I wasn't here to greet you when you came in. I was in the back feeding the pigs."

I smiled when she said 'pigs.' There were pigs here.

"I can't wait to meet them," I commented.

Beatrice was sniffing my palm. She seemed to be expecting something.

"My partner went back to the pickup," I said. "We left our bag of treats in the truck."

"Treats are good," said Helga. "Let's get in my truck to go into the sanctuary. Then we'll swing around to get your partner. We'll visit the cows first and then the pigs."

"Sounds good," I replied.

Beatrice snorted as I pulled my hand away.

"Beatrice is a Brahman cow," Helga told me as she heaved the gearshift of her green pickup. The truck was a model dating back probably two decades. Old-style locks jutted from metal doors.

"She's larger than most. Everybody thinks that Brahman cows are enormous. But the females, on average, are just the same size as the Holsteins. She's a little bigger than the rest," pointed out Helga.

We picked up Ainsley in our silver pickup parked on the shoulder of the road in front of Helga's house. Introductions were made. Helga explained to Ainsley that we had been talking about Beatrice, the Brahman cow, who greeted me.

Helga motioned with her arm and pointed to Beatrice. The cow had turned away from the fence and was trotting toward us.

"She's very affectionate," remarked Helga. I just fed her, so it's more than treats that she wants.

"Wait a minute," said Ainsley, "I brought something for her."

Ainsley reached into a large vinyl bag, rummaged around, and produced a burlap bag full of sliced apples.

I was squished in the middle of the front seat in the cab.

"Go ahead," said Ainsley, drawing back so I could reach my arm out the window.

Beatrice's lips were cool and moist against my flat hand as she nibbled on the apple slices.

Two months after Mama had died, I was still moping around the house. The farm no longer interested me. I couldn't go into the pasture, and I couldn't open my mail. The mail was mostly bills anyway.

I had told Ainsley about the cow sanctuary months ago when Candace had first told me about it. Ainsley said nothing at the time. I took this as a comment about Candace. But apparently Ainsley had enough of my moping around after Mama's passing and insisted that we take a day trip to the cow sanctuary.

I agreed, although inwardly I groaned and thought, Not more cows.

I had been curious about the sanctuary – but mostly I came because Ainsley suggested it. Ainsley had given up on job hunting and seemed happier.

Now that we were here, I was glad we had come. It was only a two-hour drive south of our farm, but it felt like a different world. There was a feeling of peace at the sanctuary, and it evoked another emotion in me that I couldn't yet identify. I just knew that it felt expansive. I had the feeling of being larger than myself and of being at peace in the world.

Plus, I really liked Helga.

"Most people think of bulls when they hear about Brahman cattle. Normally, I don't like to use the word 'cattle' because it sounds so impersonal. It's almost as bad as 'livestock,' stated Helga. "These cows aren't livestock. None should be. The cows who live here have their own personalities. They're as unique as people. They're like pets to me, but really, they're more than that. They're beings."

I nodded along with Ainsley.

A silence hung in the air, indicating that it was our turn to talk. It wasn't an uncomfortable silence, but Helga broke it.

"So, tell me what brought you here?"

She stopped talking. There was so much that I could tell her, how it had all started with Cinnamon spying on me, or how

I had nursed Spice back to health only to realize she would be sent to slaughter in a few years. I couldn't tell Helga I thought Cinnamon was trying to talk to me. Helga might think I was crazy. I had just met her and didn't want her to think I was irrational. I could tell Helga I was here because nothing made sense anymore since my Mama had passed. But if I told Helga that, I might break down crying. I didn't know her well enough to risk looking like a mess. There were many things, I could say about why we were here. But I knew with a sinking sensation that at the bottom of things, I was a traditional dairy farmer. I thought of myself as the enemy.

"Oh, we just needed a change of scenery," answered Ainsley breezily. "Plus, we're going vegan, and we heard about what you are doing, so here we are. I was wondering, Beatrice is so unusual. Where did she come from?"

I looked at Ainsley lovingly, and gratefully.

"There's a Hindu cow sanctuary about an hour away that's going out of business. The owner is retiring so he sent his cows to live at several different sanctuaries. It was hard to break up the herd but at least they are safe, and Beatrice seems to like it here."

"I've heard that Hindus worship cows," I said.

"Yes, many Hindus do worship cows. They consider cows to be the sacred caregiver. As I see it, the cow is the sacred feminine. Strict Hindus don't eat meat or animal products. Most are essentially vegans even if they don't call it that. Of course, strict Hindus also oppose the rights of women – which doesn't make sense."

Ainsley and I both nodded.

"But they are right when it comes to the sacredness of cows. You've heard the saying 'Holy Cow!' – well that goes back to the cattle cults in Northern Africa. You may have heard of the goddess Hathor in ancient Egypt. She was often represented as a cow and there is evidence that she was worshipped for nearly three thousand years."

There was silence in the cab as Helga navigated the ruts of the pasture. As we lurched in our seats, I looked out the window. There were clumps of cows here and there, standing together. Some stood close – flicking each other with their tails – the way that Cinnamon and Spice did.

There were two mama cows standing side by side with their calves at the far end of the field. "The mother cows and their calves like to keep their distance," said Helga as she followed my gaze. "I guess they feel like they are in their own little world."

"Are there just female cows here or do you have male cows, too?" interjected Ainsley.

Helga laughed. It was the kind of laugh that filled the air with the sound of chimes. It was the kind of laugh that was genuine. Even her laughter was serene. She seemed to love what she did. I tried to imagine her doing something else but couldn't.

"We call male cows bulls. Sometimes they are called steers, but that sounds too much like a steakhouse. We don't have bulls yet, but we might have some soon. I got a call from an older farmer who wants to give me two mama cows and their male calves. Before I take them, I have to build a fence in the pasture to keep the bulls and the cows separate."

Achoo. I sneezed.

"I don't have a cold," I said after I had wiped my nose on a tissue that Ainsley magically presented to me. "But sometimes I have allergies. But I have noticed in the past month since I've given up dairy that my allergies are much better."

"Dairy does tend to make people have excess mucus – not to mention what the hormones do. There are natural hormones in dairy – lactating mothers produce estrogen – plus most cows have unnatural hormones injected into them to make them grow bigger and give more milk.

I'm surprised that more people haven't woken up. Eating dairy isn't only supporting the industry that kills cows. It hurts people too."

I nodded.

"Sometimes, the tree mold is bad here," continued Helga. "We'll stay away from the forest, but you can see the trees at the back of the pasture."

I turned my head and looked in the direction where she was pointing.

"But I don't see a fence in front of the trees," I said.

"That's because the forest is part of the pasture," responded Helga. "The cows like to go back there and sit in the shade – especially when we have a hot day."

I kept looking.

"I see several shadows that look like cows!" I exclaimed.

"Oh, that's probably Robin and Cindy. Those are the ones who like to sit under the trees closest to the clearing. Unlike most Holsteins, which are black and white, Robin and Cindy are solid black. They're Black Angus cows. That's why they looked like shadows to you."

Helga certainly knew her cows.

"It sounds like all of the cows in your herd have names," remarked Ainsley.

"Of course, they do," responded Helga. "If they don't have names when they come here, I give them names. I also tell them they are safe here and are going to live out their natural life spans. A cow can live from fifteen to twenty years. I've even heard of some older than that when they die."

Helga sounded like she was reassuring herself that they could live longer. I imagined that she had certain special cows that she was especially fond of. A cow was a big pet to get attached to and fifteen to twenty years – or longer (I heard that some cows lived past twenty when they were allowed to) – was a long time.

I smiled reassuringly. I didn't have a chance to speak since Helga kept on speaking.

"We've been here long enough that several cows have died of old age. And the other cows, particularly the ones that were close to the deceased, mourn their dead like people do. I've seen cows shed tears, bellow, and search for their loved ones. When I worked on a dairy farm, I saw cows grieve for their calves for days. Boy calves on dairy farms are taken away and turned into veal. The mamas are also separated from their female calves. The mama cows are forced to go right back to milking, and their babies are brought up to be milked right after they get pregnant for the first time. It's a barbaric system. One day I couldn't do it anymore, so I quit. And here I am."

I said nothing. I was feeling extremely guilty. I wondered how many cows I had sent away to an early demise. We had always kept the cows until they were about five, because the slaughterhouses paid more for the younger ones. I had sent away more than I could count who were at least ten years away from the age they would have been if they died from natural causes – if they had been allowed to live.

Of course, this practice had started before I was an adult and in charge. Mama and Papa had sent the cows away after three milking cycles, just as their parents had done. At the thought of my parents, I swallowed a sob.

A wave a guilt washed over me again. Despite that I was hurting, I had taken many lives. I wanted things to be different, but I still felt guilty. I felt guilty because I was guilty. I had been complicit in many deaths. I had personally made the decision and signed the contracts for the cows to be sent away for a price. I had blood on my hands.

As the sole living representative of generations of dairy farmers, I was even more complicit. For a moment as this guilt enveloped me, I felt like I was drowning. Like a drowning person, I felt helpless. What was I going to do!? I felt so guilty that I could've screamed. I could have demanded that we leave the sanctuary. I could have defended the actions of Papa and Mama and their parents before them. I could've spent the ride home defending my right to the land and used that as an excuse to continue to do things as they always had been done.

Instead, I decided to come clean. There was something about this place that demanded honesty and I knew I would feel better if I told the truth.

I saw that Ainsley was going to say something and come to my rescue again.

This was noble but unnecessary. I could come to my own rescue.

"I should tell you," I confessed to Helga, "I'm a dairy farmer – a conventional dairy farmer. I ran — run — a farm that's been in my family for generations."

I watched Helga's eyes narrow as I talked. I knew she would be suspicious of me. After all, I was the enemy. But I kept talking. I told her about Cinnamon and her friend Spice – how I suspected Cinnamon was trying to talk to me and how I realized after nursing Spice back to health I had only saved her to send her to be slaughtered in a few years. I didn't care anymore if she thought I was crazy. I told her that Mama had died — that Papa had died a few years ago, that I was an only child, and that nothing made sense anymore. When I told Helga this, I didn't break down. I only suppressed a few sobs.

When I told Helga that I was extremely unhappy, she looked at me sadly.

She gave me a few moments to collect myself and then started asking me some very specific questions. I told her that my farm was a small one – twenty acres.

"How many cows do you have?" she asked.

"Forty-five," I said. "Oh, I mean thirty."

Fifteen cows had been sent away, but I tended not to think about it. I had tried to block the knowledge of this out of my mind. But the cows were old enough to be sent away to be slaughtered, and I had needed the money, so they went. Even though the slaughterhouse sent the trucks in the dead of night, it still had happened.

I felt very guilty.

When Helga asked me if the land had been passed down to me and if it was paid for free and clear, I nodded.

"There's no reason to feel bad about the past," said Helga. As she spoke her eyes widened in compassion.

"We all have regrets. But if you just feel bad about what's been done, then you're stuck in those feelings, and you can't move forward."

Helga smiled but her eyes still looked sad. I took a breath and tried to smile back, but I found myself tearing up.

Helga took a breath with me. We sat in silence.

Ainsley was silent too.

"You're not alone. Many dairy farmers are so depressed that they attempt suicide. But you can do things differently," said

Helga. She sucked in her breath as if she was worried that she had gone too far.

We were all quiet for a moment.

"You can do this," said Helga breaking the silence. "You can change things. You can make life better for the cows and yourself. It will be easier than you think it will be."

I nodded.

The only thing I didn't tell her was that Mama had left me some money. It wasn't a lot. But my parents had always been frugal so there was more than I thought there would be. There was enough to provide me with a buffer so that I could make a change. I didn't tell Helga this, because I thought it bad form to talk about inheriting money. To many, it was a sore spot. Someone else got what they thought they deserved or there was nothing when they thought there would be something. But I had never thought about the future in terms of inheriting money. I didn't expect my parents to die, and I hadn't wanted my parents to die.

While I talked, Helga's eyes widened. Finally, I said I wanted to do things differently. Helga nodded and told me I was doing the right thing and offered to provide advice and a listening ear along the way. She told me she loved what she did and she couldn't imagine doing anything else, but that it was a lot of work. In fact, she said, she worked all the time.

Suddenly I knew what the sensation was that I had been feeling – the expansiveness. It wasn't the size of the land or the azure sky above us. It wasn't that this was my favorite time of year, with the leaves starting to turn and the crickets singing.

Then it came to me. I suddenly knew what I had been feeling since I arrived. The expansiveness I felt was freedom. The cows were going to live out their natural lifetimes. They were going to live for as long as God intended. This opened the future for me too. I would have a purpose and that purpose was to stop the killing or at least part of it. Maybe it was small, but it was something.

I took a deep breath and smelled hope.

Chapter Twenty-Six

There I was standing in the pasture next to Spice. We didn't say as much, but we were waiting for Sunflower and her friend to come home.

It was Ham Sandwich's day to be the farmhand, so we knew we wouldn't be milked as much.

We didn't admit it – even to ourselves – but we were bored. At least I was. I assume that Spice was also.

Every time I saw a car go by, I looked up, but the silver pickup never turned into the drive.

"Give her some time, Sunflower's barely been gone," commented Spice.

"I'm not waiting for Sunflower," I responded, somewhat crossly. "I was just curious as to who was driving by."

"Hmmph," responded Spice.

Just to show her that I wasn't waiting for Sunflower to come home, I turned around and began grazing on a patch of tall onion grass.

"I don't know why you care. She ignored us for days," said Spice whose voice seemed to float on a breeze as she stood behind me.

I could feel Spice's tail hitting my side as she flicked away flies on her side.

She was still facing the driveway and the street.

It was particularly buggy today. I could feel the skin on my side quivering.

The flies made me feel even more irritated than I was.

"I didn't notice Sunflower ignoring us," I commented. "Even if she did, I ignored her first."

Spice's comment cut me to the bone. It must have been obvious that I was hurt the other day when Sunflower ignored us. It wasn't just me. She ignored Spice also – after nursing her back to health. Nonetheless, I wasn't going to admit to Spice, Sunflower hurt my feelings.

Spice rarely mentioned the time that she spent with Sunflower when she was sick. Spice had been well long enough that we had almost forgotten the past. We were staying in the present by insulting each other.

I still couldn't believe Sunflower had ignored us. I had spent a long time getting to know her. A friendship seemed to be budding between us. Then she dropped us – seemingly out of nowhere.

Maybe her behavior has to do with money, I thought. *Or maybe she feels guilty about her past actions – or maybe it is both.*

The thoughts seemed to come out of nowhere. It was very quiet in the pasture. The crickets hummed. The air smelled fresh. I could smell myself and the other cows and that was a good thing. A gentle breeze went by. I saw one of the first autumn leaves falling from a nearby tree. If it wasn't for the flies, it would have been a perfect day.

"I think Sunflower ignored us because she has a lot on her mind. She does a lot of things you know. She doesn't just pay attention to us," I stated.

"You're just defending her," commented Spice. "I don't know why. I was watching you and you were depressed for days after she walked right by the pasture several times without a glance in our direction."

"Excuse me?" I retorted.

"Uh. Oh. What did you do?"

I couldn't see her face since we were still facing in opposite directions, but I could just imagine Spice daintily sniffing the air.

"I didn't do anything," I replied defensively. "I was referring to your comment that you were watching me and that you knew I was depressed. First of all, you had no business watching me. Secondly, you don't know I was depressed. You're not in my body so you don't know what I'm feeling."

Spice just stared at me with her big brown eyes. Apparently, she had never thought about this.

"Of course, I can tell how you're feeling. After Sunflower ignored us, you were feeling depressed. And now I can tell you are feeling irritated."

She was right. I was feeling irritated. Maybe I was taking out my feelings of frustration about Sunflower on Spice, but Spice wasn't helping any.

"You're damn right I'm feeling irritated," I said. "You always comment on my farts even when I don't fart. You act like you never fart – like you're not part of the smell around here. Speaking for myself, I'm proud to be part of the smell. I like things that smell like me."

"That explains it," replied Spice.

"That explains what?"

"That explains why you fart so much. You're trying to fill up the air with yourself," said Spice matter-of-factly.

"I DO NOT fart that much," I replied.

"Do too," retorted Spice.

"You fart too," I replied.

"Not as much as you," Spice said. "In fact, I'm taking my life in my hooves with my head so close to your rear end."

I thought about this. Maybe she had a point. I was bigger so maybe I did fart more. But I wasn't going to admit this to her.

I felt like I might fart then. But I held it in so as not to prove her right.

"You always have to have the last word," I said instead.

"That's right," she responded.

I knew this could go on all day. Normally, I didn't mind that she had to have the last word. Her stubbornness was one of the things that I found endearing about her. It certainly seemed like she was feeling better. But for many different reasons, I was feeling angry today. So, I moved away from her into my own circle in the pasture about ten feet away. I thought I was beyond hearing distance.

"You do too fart," I said in a low mumble.

"Do not," she shot back.

I sighed. It was going to be a long day. I needed to fortify myself, so I bent my head down and grazed some more. I had already eaten the tuft of the onion grass and the grass that I found wasn't so tasty. But I pretended it was.

"Mm mm. Mm mm," I said between bites.

"The grass over here isn't so tasty," called Spice.

"Well over here it's great. I'd offer you some, but I've eaten almost all of it."

Spice wasn't buying it. She pointedly ignored me, turned around so that her rear end was close to mine and began sniffing the ground in front of her.

We grazed that way for a while in mutual irritation.

Then there was the distant sound of tires crunching against gravel in the driveway.

"Thank God," said Spice. "She's finally here. Maybe you'll stop being in a mood."

"Thank who?" I asked.

"Thank God," repeated Spice. "It's an expression I picked up from Sunflower when she was taking care of me."

"Hmmph," I replied as I turned around.

I started to run up to the fence, but then stopped myself. What if Sunflower ignored me again? I didn't want to become depressed, and I didn't want Spice to accuse me of being depressed again. I thought it best just to stand still and see what was happening.

I heard the door slam after Sunflower got out of the pickup. She stood on the passenger side and exchanged a few words with her human companion. She started to walk toward the farmhouse, but then she hesitated. She and her companion exchanged a few more words. I heard something about "dinner."

Then she walked to the wooden fence around the pasture.

"Cinnamon, Spice," she called.

I waited until she called our names a second time and then ran to greet her. Spice was by my side. We both reached our heads out under the top railing of the wooden fence and nuzzled her hands back.

I noticed a smell on her hand. Another cow?!

I knew she had a human companion and I had made my peace with that – especially since the companion had given me treats.

I knew a house cat lived with her. I could smell the cat on her. That's what cats do. They spread their smell around. I certainly wasn't going to take that seriously.

Now I find out she has a secret cow friend somewhere?!

"Wait a minute," she said and reached into the burlap bag at her side.

"I saved you some treats," she said, holding her hand out.

Mm mm. Pieces of carrots and a few apple slices!

Spice and I gobbled down our treats.

I thought briefly of that *OTHER* cow. *There were probably more apple slices, and SHE probably ate the good ones.* But then I banished the thought. What Sunflower said next changed everything. I had never seen her so sincere. I could tell she meant what she said.

"I'm sorry I walked past you and ignored you that other day," she said as she rubbed my nose. Then she stroked Spice's ears. "I was afraid I wouldn't be able to keep my promise to you – my favorite girls. But on my trip today I realized I can keep my promise and I MUST – so that you and the others never have to go away."

I forgave her immediately. I was so angry about the other cow whom I had smelled, I had thought about not letting Sunflower pet me. But it felt nice when the farmer stroked me, so I let her do it. It felt so good that I decided to forgive the other cow. That other cow, whoever she was, had led Sunflower home to us.

CINNAMON: A dairy cow's (and her farmer's) path to freedom

I looked up and saw a big tear falling from Sunflower's eye.

I saw it and then it was blurry because big tears had formed in my eyes.

Janet Mason

Chapter Twenty-Seven

Tranquil music hung in the air. The piano player – I couldn't see his face, only the back of his collar-length walnut-colored hair – sat in the corner of the large room. The high ceiling made the room seem spacious. Maybe the piano music made the room seem larger also. I had the sensation of soaring with the notes.

I had seen a flyer at church on a light green piece of paper for a "Thanks Living" vegan potluck and had taken it home. The people at church were always talking about seeing their children and grandchildren on the holidays, but I didn't have that kind of extended family. I didn't feel bad I didn't have children or grandchildren. I didn't feel like I didn't have anyone. I felt extra sad this holiday because I didn't have Mama, but I had Ainsley. And I had my cow family. I also had the joy of knowing I could do things differently. I was grateful.

Ainsley and I used to go to the home to see Mama on Thanksgiving. The Home's dining room was always open and on Thanksgiving, they served turkey with all the trimmings. We always had two pieces of pie, pumpkin, and pecan, with whipped cream for dessert.

Ainsley picked up the flyer from where I left it on the old wooden coffee table, read it, and insisted we were going.

"Now is the perfect time to start new traditions," Ainsley announced, "and this sounds perfect. I'll make either my Greek Goddess Bowl or peanut noodles."

So that's how we ended up coming to the potluck even though I had announced earlier I was going to spend the day of Thanksgiving in bed watching old movies. Then I told Ainsley I didn't believe in Thanksgiving anyway because we had stolen the land from the Native people and there was nothing to celebrate.

I guess I was a little depressed about the holidays. Just because I was right about its origins didn't mean I couldn't still be depressed. Plus, Ainsley was starting a business cooking plant-based dishes for other people. We figured we could pick up some new recipes at the potluck and maybe even find some new customers.

So instead of dreading the holidays, I had been looking forward to this day and the "Thanks Living" potluck. It was exciting to do something new. For one thing, the "Thanks Living" potluck had no memories associated with it, which would make me sad.

Ainsley and I sat at a round table in the back of the large lunchroom in the high school that was also used for community events. People trickled in. I saw Candace standing in the front of the room talking to a woman I knew from church. I guessed that the woman had dropped the flyers off. I refrained from waving Candace over to our table because I knew that Ainsley tried to avoid her.

The large room was filled with round tables with six or seven-place settings. Gradually all the tables were filled. There must have been close to a hundred people in the room. The woman who organized the event said a few words about how this was the second vegan potluck she was hosting and how this year she was proud to have Dr. Will Tuttle as our guest who was going to speak later after we ate. She said speaking would give him a break from playing the piano. Then she told us that going vegan – almost ten years ago – had changed her life but that she wanted to hear from us. She asked us to stand and introduce ourselves briefly from our places.

Starting from the table in front of the room, people began standing and introducing themselves. When people talked about the health benefits of going vegan, it was rather amazing.

"I used to have heart disease," said a tall older man wearing a blue and white checkered shirt. He tugged at one of his long sleeves as he spoke. He was thin and wore gray plastic-rimmed spectacles. "I heard the only diet that could reverse heart disease was a vegan diet. When I first heard this, I didn't believe it. But" – the man shrugged – "I figured what did I have to lose. So, I tried it. Now, I have more energy than ever and after three years on a plant-based diet, my doctor declared me free of my former heart condition."

The next person was the wife of the man who had just spoken. Her mass of short brown curls shook as she spoke. She said that she wasn't entirely vegan herself, but she ate lots of vegan food and was grateful to have her husband.

Then another woman at their table said she became vegan when she was diagnosed with diabetes several months ago and slowly through her plant-based diet and a new exercise routine of walking she was getting better and, with her physician's help, she hoped to be able to give up her medications soon.

By the time we got to the end of the second table, I had heard about many health issues. One woman's joint pain had magically disappeared after a year of being on a plant-based diet. Another mentioned his chronic sinus infections had gone away, and another person slept better.

It was a little hard to believe all the health claims at first. But then I said to myself that most health issues are caused by high cholesterol – and where does cholesterol come from? I'd read it mostly comes from the saturated fat in meat, fowl, seafood, and dairy products but that the body produces all the cholesterol it needs. So, it makes sense that if you eliminate all animal-based products, you would lower your cholesterol and have less chance of diseases related to high cholesterol.

Many people also talked about the treatment of the animals.

An older woman went on and on about an article she had read about the mistreatment of animals. She went on for so long and in such graphic detail that people started shushing her and saying that she shouldn't be talking about this when we were just about to eat.

Another woman talked about the fact she started eating a vegan diet for health reasons and then learned about the treatment of the animals and that the vegan diet is good for the planet.

"With these three things, becoming vegan seems like a no-brainer." She smiled as she spoke. Wisps of brown hair framed her long thin face.

I hadn't heard much about veganism affecting the planet and made a mental note to learn more.

When it was my time to introduce myself, I was dizzy with all I had heard.

"I've been on a plant-based diet for a few months and already feel the difference," I said adding, "It feels great to be healthy."

Finally, we got in line for food, section by section. I looked to the front left of the room and saw long rectangular tables with plastic tablecloths laden with dishes of food.

Smiles were exchanged. Lips were licked. This was the main event – the reason we had come.

When I reached the front of the line, I filled half my plate with couscous which had a dark brown tint smelling like cinnamon, chickpeas with mango curry sauce (this was the dish Ainsley decided to bring that morning), and some fresh leafy greens.

The food seemed to shimmer in its pureness, adding to the light in the room. Everyone seemed happy.

I sat down back at my table and dug into my food.

"The mango chickpeas are wonderful," I commented to Ainsley.

"They sure are," said the man next to me.

He told me his name was David.

I turned toward him and chatted for a while. Overhead light glinted from the bald patch on the dome of his head. His short dark hair matched his black-rimmed glasses. He was older than me – probably in his late forties. He had been a librarian specializing in Boolean searches.

"It all ended with the advent of Google and the other search engines. I had to retrain and became a reference librarian," he told me.

So, it is possible to teach an old dog new tricks, I thought.

I was thinking of myself, of course. Most people are.

He confided in me that this was his second feast of the day – the first was turkey with the trimmings at his adult daughter's house (no grandchildren yet). Then he told me that he wasn't a vegan (yet) but sometimes felt guilty after he had eaten a burger because he knew he was coming to a vegan potluck because his vegetarian wife wanted to go.

"But the hamburgers sure are good," he commented.

"The food here is good too," I said, smiling back at him.

I didn't say anything negative because … well … who am I to judge?

I certainly had followed the program and eaten lots of meat in my lifetime.

I hadn't yet told him that I was – or had been – a dairy farmer.

People finished their dinners and stood up to get dessert. There was another long table off to the side that was laden with delicious-looking desserts. I decided that I wouldn't eat dessert.

Vegan desserts were different. No animal products were used. But I figured that sugar is basically sugar – even when it comes from beets and dates. I was still watching my weight. Although, it no longer felt like the most important thing to me since I had lost a little weight, and my feet didn't hurt anymore. I figured that I would just reach the weight that was healthy for my body and stay there.

Just then the doctor got up to talk. I thought at first that he was a medical doctor, but it turned out that he was the other kind of doctor – of philosophy. He had written a book called *The World Peace diet*.

He talked about how when we eat animal products, we absorb the energy of suffering; that when we eliminate dairy, we are no longer ingesting hormones which manipulate human hormones and too often cause disease. He mentioned there is no such thing as "hormone-free" dairy since all pregnant cows naturally produce hormones in their milk. "There is only milk with no added hormones," he said. He talked about the fact cows know when they are being led to slaughter and that people who eat meat, absorb the adrenaline which is released in their bodies.

When I thought about the animals, I felt guilty again. But this time the guilt I felt about the past only made me more determined to make the changes I needed to. I felt stronger knowing that I was part of a movement – based on a community.

Then he talked about how cows fart and burp methane gas and that this is a major contributor to global greenhouse emissions which cause climate change.

When he said that this methane gas from farm animals was higher than all transportation industries put together, Ainsley did a double take.

Hmmm. I didn't know cows had a gas problem, I thought.

He mentioned that there were a number of problems with eating chicken besides the suffering of the animal. He mentioned studies have shown chicken has as much saturated fat as red meat. Then he emphasized the oceans are overfished and talked about dead zones and how we are eating the toxins that are dumped into the oceans when we eat fish or shellfish.

I looked across the room at Candace when he said this. She was smiling and nodding. Either she had changed her ways and no longer made exceptions for shellfish, or she was just agreeing with him in the moment. I suspected I would find out the next time we had dinner together.

He finished his talk by quoting the ancient Greek philosopher Pythagoras who said: "*'As long as men massacre animals, they will kill each other.'*"

What he said made so much sense that my mind was swirling. I got up to get in line to buy his book but remembered my new friend David sitting next to me.

CINNAMON: A dairy cow's (and her farmer's) path to freedom

I sat back down and wished him luck with everything.

"I never got to ask," he said, "what do you do?"

So, I told him that I was – or had been – a dairy farmer. I told him the farm had been in my family for generations.

"A dairy farmer?!" the man replied. "That's not unusual around these parts, but it's unusual you're here!"

Then I told him that my awareness had changed. I told him that Cinnamon the cow had pushed me in the right direction.

He looked a little guilty. Just a short while ago, he had talked about how good a hamburger tastes to him.

I sat with him in the silence of our shared guilt.

Then I told him what Ainsley and I were planning on doing.

Chapter Twenty-Eight

"I haven't felt this good since I was a heifer," I said.

"Your legs aren't as spindly, commented Spice.

"I know I'm not as young as I was," I replied. "That's not what I meant. I meant now that we aren't being milked by the machines, I finally feel like a cow should feel and the last time I felt that way was when I was a calf – before I was sexually mature and able to give birth and was then milked by the machines."

"Was this before you knew what would ultimately become of us?" asked Spice. She looked at me gravely with her big brown eyes.

I was silent for a moment and shared her serious look. "I really can't remember – but maybe it was."

The moment passed.

"I was wondering – how should a cow feel?" asked Spice. "Hungry?"

She didn't sound sarcastic. She seemed curious. Spice seemed to be asking how she should feel. It seemed absurd to me, to ask how you should feel.

I absentmindedly flicked a fly away from my side with my tail while I thought about how I should respond to Spice. Finally, I thought of something.

"I can't tell you, how you should feel," I replied as I looked out over the pasture. It was a sunny day, but a dark cloud was headed in our direction. I sniffed the air. It smelled moist. It would probably rain later. Most likely, we would have to go back to the barn. It wasn't so smelly anymore since the cheerful young people had shown up to clean it. They talked to us and petted us too.

"I'm just telling you about my experience. I feel great. Knowing that we are no longer on the schedule of the milking machines, I can finally relax."

"Really? You can relax? Aren't you worried about the future?" asked Spice.

"I'm finally not worried about the future. I believe Sunflower. She said that you and me and the others would be safe from now on. That means we won't be sent away." I flicked my tail again. The itch on my side went away.

Hah, I got him, I thought, thinking of the fly.

"You believe the farmer?"

Spice was starting to sound like herself again.

"Sure, I believe her," I replied. "Sunflower had never sounded so sincere."

"She might have felt that way in the moment," Spice commented.

"In the moment?!" I cried. "Whatever do you mean?"

"I mean that the farmer might temporarily have had a change of heart, and she might have forgotten all about us when she walked away." Spice enunciated her words as if she were talking to a calf who didn't yet understand the ways of the world.

I had once been such a calf. I loved humans then. I was lonely and they came and brought us treats and stroked our noses. But then I found out the collective fate of all the cows! At first, I couldn't believe it. It seemed such an act of betrayal by the people who came and petted our soft noses. Sometimes they even brought their children with their little pudgy arms and legs. They were so small. I could tell they were good-hearted, just like us. Then it would have been impossible to even think it. Even in retrospect, it's hard to believe that some of those children ate us.

I refused to believe that everyone ate us then. That's how naïve I was.

I reflected on my thoughts and the fact that now, I believed Sunflower.

"I believed Sunflower when she said we would be safe," I said. I felt like I was reassuring myself by saying this.

"It wouldn't be the first time that humans made empty promises to us," pointed out Spice as she moved away from me. I heard a burping sound when she opened her mouth. So, she did have gas, I thought. It just came out the front and not the back. She didn't bother to say, "excuse me."

I decided to ignore her comment and her behavior, too.

"I heard the farmer just bought a piglet down to live in the old pig pen. I also heard that she named the pig Wilbur. It seems that humans find baby pigs to be extremely cute. Maybe she's switching her allegiance from us to the pig," continued Spice.

"She NAMED the pig?" I was incredulous. Then I said, "Wilbur seems like an odd name for a pig."

"That's what I heard." Spice had a triumphant gleam in her eye.

Holding this information back – knowledge that was new to me – must have been killing her.

"Still," I replied, "Just because she has a new piglet doesn't mean that she isn't going to keep her promise to us."

I chewed my cud as I thought of something.

"Maybe someone gave her the piglet," I added. "Maybe she is just keeping the piglet here for a friend."

"Then why would she name him?" Spice sounded snarky.

Maybe the piglet was already named Wilbur, I thought.

But I didn't say anything because I could tell from Spice's tone, that she thought she was right and, moreover, that it was important to her. Plus, she had to have the last word. This could go on forever.

Why bother, I thought and changed the topic.

"I was telling you how I feel now we aren't being milked by the machines on a schedule. I also noticed I feel freer after they took the yellow chips out of our ears."

"Yellow chips?"

"Yes, the big yellow chips. They contain the hormones that made us eat more so that we would grow fatter and produce more milk. The chips were behind our ears. You must have seen them on other cows. How could you not have noticed?"

"I just realized that I do have a dim memory of them. The farmhand came around to us in our slots and with a noisy and cold metal stapler and put those chips behind our ears. It was a while ago, and my memory of it is murky. They do so many things to us I tend to blank out my memories."

"Those yellow chips injected growth hormones into our bodies," I said with some authority. I had overheard the farmhands talking and repeated what I heard. "The growth hormones made us hungrier, so we ate more and then we produced more milk."

"That's why I blocked it out of my memory," grumbled Spice. "Blah. Blah. Blah. It's all about producing more milk."

I was silent for a moment. She did have a point. It was all about us providing them with milk. Even if it was over, it wasn't fair. But I didn't want to encourage her to be more negative. So, I didn't say anything.

"My point is that since they took the hormone chips out of our ears, I feel better. I am less hungry, so I am eating less. I can feel myself getting full and then I stop."

"Now you really are imagining things," said Spice rolling her eyes and pawing the ground with her two front hooves. "The hormones from those chips are probably in our bloodstreams and it will take months or years before we feel the difference."

I was quiet for a moment. Spice had a good head for scientific things. I was more intuitive and tended to ignore science (but I was often correct). Spice was probably right about the hormone chips releasing growth hormones into our bloodstreams.

"You're probably right," I said. "But I do feel better. I feel freer like I said, and I feel less hungry. I think I took off a few pounds. I feel friskier."

I meant the last part but right then the bodily impulse that I couldn't deny was pressing down on my bladder. I had to pee, badly.

"Excuse me," I said and began to amble swiftly to the corner of the pasture.

"Why?! What did you do?" asked Spice as she tentatively sniffed the air.

"Don't worry," I answered. "I just have to pee."

I was already in the corner with my hind quarters toward the back fence and my front facing Spice. I was too preoccupied with peeing to tell Spice what I usually told her – that she farted too. I did feel a little guilty about the fact I had lied about just having to pee. Usually, after I peed a little poof of air came out of my sphincter. I hoped it was a silent one.

Pretty soon, I felt the pee gushing out of me and all I could think of was how good it felt to let all the liquid go. Then I farted.

Phfft.

Spice didn't give any indication that she heard it.

"Boy that felt good," I said when I came back to my space next to Spice in the pasture.

"It seems like you are feeling very good today. Good for you!" said Spice.

Her eyes gleamed at me. I beamed back at her. It was a pleasure standing in this field with my best friend. The sky was still blue. There were wispy white clouds and here and there a pile of colorful leaves – red, gold, and brown – lay under a tree, half-naked of leaves.

A soft breeze blew and scattered one of the piles. Colors swirled. The smell of fermentation was in the air. The air was warm. It felt like spring. But I could tell from the leaves that autumn was here. A curled leaf spiraled down from a nearby tree. I could see red on the inside of the leaf and brown on the edges. It slowly floated down to the ground where it would become earth again. Maybe it would grow another tree.

It was a beautiful day. But then I said something which may have been the thing that ruined the good feeling.

I continued to beam at Spice. It was true that in the past I had wondered if change was possible. But now change was in the air. It was undeniable. It shimmered like the patch of golden leaves that still clung to the top of a nearby tree.

Things were going to be different. I heard the banging of construction coming from the farmhouse. Usually, I found loud noises to be jarring but this time the noise reassured me that things were going to be better.

"It's a gorgeous day," I said to Spice. "I believe Sunflower. We are safe here."

Spice narrowed her eyes and moved away from me.

"We'll see," she grumbled.

Chapter Twenty-Nine

"I've heard that plants have feelings too which puts a whole new slant on vegetarians," the older woman sitting next to me snickered. "Don't you think? Well, I do and ..."

We were in the church basement for coffee hour after the service. Folding metal chairs lined the wide white brick walls. I was sitting there first with an empty chair next to me and Doris, one of the oldest women (and the most opinionated) in the congregation sat down next to me and started talking. Doris was a nonstop talker. I would describe her as someone who thought she was liberal, but she was – for the most part – closeminded to new ideas. I knew that answering her back was like conversing with the wind. Or maybe it was more like batting my head against a brick wall. At least if I were conversing with the wind, there was a possibility of my words being heard somewhere. I knew this but was brimming with new information with all the reading I had done on veganism.

"That's true. I do believe plants have feelings." I raised my voice over Doris who was trying to interrupt me.

"But there are more than three million starving children in the world and if they were fed the grain raised to feed cattle, then they wouldn't be starving. The Buddhists say that when people eat animals, they are eating the flesh of the starving children," I continued without stopping. I did this so I could get my thoughts out. But as I spoke, I knew I was being as bad as Doris with her nonstop talking.

Doris looked at me strangely. I don't know if she was more surprised by what I said or the fact I had interrupted her.

"Oh, the Buddhists," she said dismissively. "I heard there are some that only eat three grains of rice a day. Buddhist smuddhist, that's what I say. As my mother always said…"

She was launching into a monologue. I knew she had important things to say I hadn't heard before, but I had a hard time listening when people talked on and on. I still tend to check out when this happens. So, Doris had said a lot to me I didn't take in. But I knew Doris was interested in anything related to climate change because, as she had told me, her grandchildren were going to live through the worst of it. I also knew that she was negative and a nonstop talker and that she had to be right. I couldn't take anymore.

But I knew the best way to deal with someone was to take the advice of watering the good seeds. Since it didn't seem like anything good would come out of this nonstop talking, I excused myself to get some more food. I helped myself to some grapes that were such a deep red they were almost purple. The grapes were the first thing on the long table that I could eat. The table was laden with small dishes of cubed yellow cheese, crackers, pepperoni in a bowl, along with donuts in a white box and pieces of pie still in a disposable metal pie pan. I was avoiding sweets, and the desserts on the table weren't vegan anyway. I knew that Ainsley brought a vegan dish, but I hadn't seen it yet.

I also knew that the best way to influence someone to try new vegan food was to offer them something yummy that was vegan. I made a mental note to bring one of Ainsley's new dishes to church. I would offer some to Doris next time instead of trying to talk to her.

I was beyond feeling any cravings for the food I used to find yummy and pop in my mouth. My entire taste pallet had changed. I no longer wanted to eat suffering or support an industry I was getting out of. Also, it seemed like I was getting fuller faster. I could no longer eat as much as I used to.

I had no regrets. I looked down at my plate. The grapes on my plate looked good.

Then I walked to the other side of the room and sat down with an empty chair next to me. Who would sit down next to me? It would be a surprise.

Ainsley was here for a change and was across the room handing out flyers for our new plant-based meals-to-go business.

I picked a dark red grape from the bunch on my plate and popped it into my mouth. One followed another. Sweetness exploded in my mouth. The grapes were juicy too. I had thought I would have to get a drink, but I wasn't thirsty anymore.

I didn't think the people at church would be that receptive to veganism. After all, churchgoers tended to be conventional people and conventional people tended to want to do what they had always done and what their parents had always done.

But as Ainsley had pointed out, everyone ate some vegan food (vegetables, fresh or not) and once they found out how good it tasted and how much better it made them feel, they were more likely to eat a plant-based diet. Plus, many of the people in the congregation were getting older and had health issues. At the very least, they were bound to eat a healthier diet once they learned a few new recipes and changed some old habits.

I looked down at the long table before me and saw that there were more plant-based dishes. Some of them had little index cards in front of them with the ingredients listed. One index card read "Quinoa and Black Beans." Past a dish labeled turkey meatballs, there was a ridged ceramic bowl that contained some interesting-looking noodles. I picked up the index card leaning against it and read the dish contained cauliflower pasta with toasted walnuts, parsley, garlic, and onions. I helped myself to a few spoons of quinoa with black beans. I knew that Ainsley had brought that dish.

I was finding that the people in the church had noticed that I had taken off some weight and looked healthier than I had in years. They remarked on this and then asked how my foot was doing. I told them the planter fasciitis seemed to have gone away and that I had a new regiment of walking and stretching. I had recently added the stretching.

Even Doris had noticed that I was looking healthier. That's how we got on the subject of veganism which ended in "Buddhist smuddhist."

The bottom line was that the people here – even Doris – wanted the best for me. That's why I came here on most Sundays.

I wanted the best for them also. That's why I told them about my vegan diet and how it was working for me. If they became defensive – some did – I chalked their behavior off to the impression I had that they might be feeling guilty. Most people would feel guilty after putting a face to their dinner.

Maybe I got away from the few people (like Doris) who were too much for me to deal with, but I tried not to judge anyone because who was I to judge?

I agreed with Candace that when it comes to veganism there are no bad people.

For years, I believed what I was taught to believe – that animals were here to serve us. Specifically, I had believed they were here to help us make a living and to be eaten by humans. I had believed the Big Lie: that I needed to eat dairy and meat for protein when protein was in everything we ate.

I was a former dairy farmer, and I was a living testament to the fact that change is possible.

People could change their thoughts, their ways, and their destinies.

As I finished the quinoa and black beans and then the rest of the grapes on my plate, I started thinking about the sermon. When the minister said that we must learn to love our neighbor as ourselves, I started thinking. The cows were my closest neighbors. Then there was Wilbur, my new piglet. The Bible said to "Love your neighbor" not "eat your neighbor."

I had always been interested in St. Francis of Assisi, the thirteenth-century Italian Catholic friar who became associated with animals and is often depicted as having a halo and letting a dove perch on his open hand. I heard somewhere he was known to refer to animals as his brothers and sisters.

"What are you thinking about?"

I looked up and saw the friendly face of Bill, an older man with a boxy face and short gray hair whom I often talked to.

He asked, so I told him. I hoped that I wasn't as verbose as Doris. I hesitated a little when I talked. I had told myself I wasn't going to tell anyone in the congregation what I had planned. I was afraid that someone would tell me that I couldn't do it. I was afraid word would get around and that I wouldn't do what I said I was going to do.

I thought I was afraid of the criticism of others but, really, I was afraid that I wouldn't live up to my own expectations.

Bill nodded and encouraged me to talk so I did. I told him what we were planning to do.

Janet Mason

Chapter Thirty

(Two years later)

I hummed to myself as I took a little walk to my organic garden at the far end of the property. I usually weeded and staked when we were in season, but it was late fall and all I had to do was to check on the garden and pick any end-of-the-season vegetables that had ripened. Far in the distance, the last brown leaves clung to an oak. On my last walk – less than a week ago – I had gone as far as the tree and admired the crackly brown many-fingered leaves it had dropped. Several weeks ago, I had listened to the plop, plop, plop of acorns dropping as I gardened.

CINNAMON: A dairy cow's (and her farmer's) path to freedom

Today, just as I had hoped, three late tomatoes had ripened on a bedraggled vine. I plucked the fruits and put them in an empty burlap bag. Ainsley would be happy to hear that we had fresh tomatoes. We would have them for lunch or dinner later in the day. I had placed the other burlap bag on the muddy ground behind me. It bulged with apple slices and cubed carrots.

I walked back to the pasture – or sanctuary – as I kept forgetting to call it. Cinnamon and Spice and the others would live out their natural lifespans here. From the distance, I could see the morning sun behind the cows. As I walked closer, their perky ears seemed to grow larger. The sun illuminated the tiny bright hairs bristling out from their ears. I stood outside the wooden fence and inhaled the air of the sunny day so deeply that it seemed to reach the soles of my feet. I took a moment to marvel at the nature of change. It was happening all around us whether we welcomed it or not. One unwitting turn could shape your entire future. My poor health and my aching foot of several years ago turned me in the direction of having more compassion for Cinnamon and Spice and ultimately for the rest of the cows – and the ones who had yet to come and live here.

I still felt bad about having to sell my old hog. But the new pig, Wilbur, had grown very big and had his own pen in the back of the pasture. It was hard to believe just two years ago I had brought him home as a piglet. The farmer who sold him to me told me he was an American Yorkshire pig. He wasn't fully grown yet, but he was the size of a small child – a child with a snout and floppy ears. The American Yorkshire pigs grew to be around six feet long. So, in two to three years, when Wilbur was fully grown, he would be the length of a tall person.

I just heard from another farmer who was going out of business, and another pig – about the same age as Wilbur – might be coming to live here. The farmer was brokenhearted about having to sell his family farm but relieved that his pig, whom he had grown attached to, had a safe place to come and live. I didn't have room for all the farmer's cattle. He had almost as many as I had. But he was farming them out to different sanctuaries. A few might come to live here.

He was broke and wanted to sell the property before he lost it. He was also appalled at his past behavior. His family had farmed for generations. But suddenly he had a change of heart that started with the pig he was giving me. He couldn't eat pork products anymore and then he couldn't eat beef. He didn't know what he was going to do next, but he wanted to get out of the industry of suffering. His face was lined. I could tell he was used to suppressing his emotions. But when I told him that this was a sanctuary and his piglet would live out his natural lifespan, I could see he was pleased. His smile was like sunlight shining through a crack in stone.

I took another deep breath and gave myself credit for somehow pulling it all together and most of all for having the faith in myself and Ainsley. We did it. After two years, we were still just scraping by. But the money that Mama left me was enough to pay the taxes for a few years. We wove the rest together patchwork the way that farmers often do. The bed and breakfast brought in some income. We had gotten some donations for our work in the sanctuary. I had rented out some land to another farmer who was raising organic vegetables. The sale of the organic vegetables we raised helped also. In addition to cooking for our guests, Ainsley still cooked vegan dishes for people within driving distance and I delivered. We were always busy. Busy but happy.

It was Helga who suggested I rent out land to another farmer – providing that they only used the land to grow organic vegetables. "You can always use the land for yourself in a few years – when you expand and start to have more cows," she had said. After she said this, I remembered Mama and Papa had made the same suggestion to rent out the land. Mama and Papa had also suggested I might want to run a bed and breakfast. When I told Helga that we were starting a vegan bed and breakfast on our sanctuary, she said that "it sounds like paradise." Helga was always so positive, and she was right.

When I was running a traditional dairy farm, we were just scraping by also. Besides, the local dairy was paying less for fresh unpasteurized milk, which came from the cows. The writing was on the wall.

At the vegetable stand, I talked to a wife of a dairy farmer. She said she heard what I was doing and hoped it worked out for me. She seemed so genuine when she spoke that later when I reflected she was probably just glad to have less competition, I felt bad. Maybe she really did wish me well. I wished her well also. I no longer believed in using cows – or any animals – for human consumption, but I really did wish my neighbors the best. I knew life was hard for farmers. I also sensed many loved their farm animals in their own way and that they would change in their own time.

I was able to save and planned to eventually buy the land behind the pasture with the line of trees where Mama and Papa's ashes were scattered. The cows would love it back there in the shade.

I loved being part of the change, part of the way things would be done in the future – part of something that was so much larger than myself and my little sanctuary.

I unlatched the wooden gate and walked into the old pasture. As I took the burlap bag from my shoulder, I was surrounded by my new friends Caramel and Cocoa. Sundae (who was born on a Sunday) nosed her black and white face next to them. Star (who I had named long ago for the white star in the middle of her back forehead) came up and stood behind me. Like many of the others I was there at her birth and remember her standing on her spindly legs in the far stall in the barn.

The cows nuzzled my hands as I fed them cubed carrots and apple slices. I felt their moist lips and their warm breath on my hands. I took a breath of the same air that they breathed and felt as if we were all one. I was closer to them now, because there was no longer any guilt between us.

I was no longer afraid to walk among the cows in the pasture. I knew the cows and their temperaments. Since I had stopped using the milking machines, there was no more head butting and no need to use the chains to hold the cows in place. I suspected it helped that the barn was cleaner. Plus, we built an addition to the barn and the cows now had more room to spread out. Several more young people had heard what we were doing, and they came and volunteered each week to clean out the barn. So, the barn was less smelly.

Jimmy still came in a few times a week to handle the heavy work such as tilling the fields. But I had let the other farmhand, Bob, go. Jimmy said that now he has a lot less work to redo. I felt bad about firing Bob, but I knew that's what I had to do to save the lives of the cows. After all, it all depended on me reducing expenses. Bob had snorted when I told him that I was turning the farm into a sanctuary. Then he smirked as if to say my idea would fail. I guess he knew what was coming. When I told him that I was sorry, but I had to let him go, he just sat there, poker faced as if he had no emotions. Then when he was leaving, he spit loudly and slammed his car door hard.

I heard him but didn't respond. My cows were free, and I felt freer.

Cinnamon and Spice were in the back of the field with their calves trailing behind them. They had been impregnated before I started the sanctuary and their calves had drunk their mothers' milk. Both of their calves were female, so I didn't have to build a fence for a separate area for the males. But I might do that in the future. Helga mentioned she has a separate fenced in field for the males and that's something I might want to consider in the future.

As the cows finished their treats, they looked up at me with their big brown eyes.

"You had your treats. Now you'll have to wait for feeding time," I said.

The cows backed away. It wasn't the first time I had the feeling that they could understand what I was saying.

I walked up the slight incline toward the gate.

Big blue squares sat on pallets next to the barn. Bales of hay were covered with a blue tarp. It was work that usually I would leave for Jimmy, but now that I had been vegan for several years, I felt stronger. I had more energy. Besides, Jimmy was off this week. I decided to get a hand truck and bring the bales of hay into the barn myself. Just as I was walking over to the hand truck leaning against the white cement wall of the barn, I heard a car turning into the drive. The sound of tires on cinders was followed by the gravel spurt of another car. I looked up and saw that they had arrived.

It was Dr. Holt, the large animal veterinarian, who I had come to know as Jean during recent months. She was a steady customer of Ainsley's home cooked vegan meals. Fortunately, I hadn't had to visit her recently for any of the cows.

She had the rest of the group with her. They lined up at the wooden fence and began singing.

Every song they sang had the word moon in it. Just for fun, they dragged out the word and said "moo" instead.

They sang "I'm being followed by a moo;" "Fly me to the moo;" "Moo light serenade" and ended with "Moo River."

In the short time that they had been singing, the cows gathered in the middle of the field and looked up at the group expectantly.

"I noticed that Cinnamon and Spice and their little ones came from their corner to listen to us," said Jean. She beamed at me.

I beamed back.

She had saved Spice's life. I wondered if Spice remembered. In many ways, Dr. Holt – I mean Jean – had set me on my journey that began with knowing others became attached to their cows also. Knowing that others felt this way too, made it okay for me.

"They must be attracted to the oxytocin that we emitted," observed Jean.

"Oxy – what?"

"Oxytocin, the hormone," replied Jean. "It's produced in humans when they give birth and then it comes from human babies. That's why people feel so good when they hold babies. They're breathing in the oxytocin. Animals must have the same hormone and their babies, too. We're all animals, after all."

I nodded my head in agreement.

"I just read choruses also produce this hormone when they sing together," commented Jean.

"That makes sense," I replied. "It must be because of the act of creation. When people sing together, they are creating a new sound – a new vibration."

Jean nodded sagely.

I turned and looked down at the field. The cows were still gathered, and they looked at us expectantly. I surmised they were expecting snacks after their entertainment.

After we gave the cows their treats, we headed into the house where Ainsley had prepared a Sunday supper for us. I recognized some of the people from church and others from the vegan "Thanks Living" potlucks.

I sat down next to a young man with his mahogany brown hair tied up in a bun. He told me he owned a dairy farm that had been in his family for generations.

"I have three brothers," he said. "But I'm the one who stuck around, so now I'm the one who is running the farm. I always did get attached to the animals, but now things are ... different for me ... something inside me snapped. I stopped eating meat and dairy and I really don't want to send away any more animals."

He told me he had gone vegan and wanted to create a sanctuary out of his farm also.

"How did you do it?" he asked.

I looked at his piercing brown eyes intently.

"It won't be easy," I said. "But you'll be immensely happy that you did it."

Then I began telling him my story.

About the Author

Cinnamon: a dairy cow's (and her farmer's) path to freedom is Janet Mason's third novel from Adelaide Books. Her novels *THEY, a biblical tale of secret genders* and *The Unicorn, The Mystery* were published by Adelaide Books in 2018 and 2020 respectively. Her book *Tea Leaves, a memoir of mothers and daughters* (Bella Books; 2012) was chosen by the American Library Association for its 2013 Over the Rainbow List. Her novel *Loving Artemis, an endearing tale of revolution, love, and marriage* was published by Thorned Heart Press in 2022. She is a lay minister for the Unitarian Universalists of Mt. Airy in Philadelphia and her talk which includes an excerpt from *Cinnamon* and was given on International Pig Day—can be found at Pig Day Revisited — #GoVeganForLent or just #GoVegan #amreading | Janet Mason, author (wordpress.com)